The Gloves of Virtue

The Gloves of Virtue

By Montgomery Phister

Rev. 1
"I hate the bigots—the deceitful race,
Of hypocrites of manner, insolents
Who don their virtues with their white kid gloves."

From ***The Cup and the Lips***
By *Alfred de Musset, 1810-1857*

iUniverse, Inc.
Bloomington

The Gloves of Virtue

iUniverse books may be ordered through booksellers or by contacting:

iUniverse
1663 Liberty Drive
Bloomington, IN 47403
www.iuniverse.com
1-800-Authors (1-800-288-4677)

ISBN: 978-1-4697-8962-0 (sc)
ISBN: 978-1-4697-8963-7 (ebk)

Printed in the United States of America

iUniverse rev. date: 03/01/2012

Dedicated to my beloved wife
Melinda Miles Phister
1944-2009

1988

CHAPTER 1

Monday Morning

I eased the Ford over into the right-hand lane and took the off ramp. We were in the country—houseless hills skewered by the freeway. At the boulevard stop there was a small sign pointing left: La Aldea, 11 miles

"I suppose it isn't," Abigail said. "There aren't many any more." Before we left home this morning I had visited the dictionary, and knew that La Aldea meant hamlet, or village.

You have to get used to Abigail. Conversation with her may sound a little like a puzzle, for she skips over things when she knows that you're with her—that your thoughts are meshed with hers. Many of her sentences won't pass muster with an English major. She talks like she thinks. So I replied to her many small towns, though she'd just said 'many'.

"There are still a few here and there," I said, "though not so many close to L.A." We were pulling off into the mountains north-west of the city, just inside Ventura County. "Of course, California place names often don't mean what they say," I reminded her. "Like Thousand Oaks has been cut down to make room for houses, and there hasn't been a seal on Seal Beach for years, and Lakewood has neither a lake nor a wood. And how many angels will you find in Los Angeles?"

"Thousands," she replied. "Audrey and Caro and Marie and Evelyn, and others we know and other we don't." Abigail's sympathy for the unorthodox, her love for the world's consolers, and her annoying and uncanny gift for seeing into people, have provided us with an eclectic crowd of friends. Many of them, like Abigail herself, seem close to whatever heaven there is. Audrey is raising six adopted children. Caro is a nurse whose sympathy is as healing as penicillin. Marie is a call girl, and uses her excess profits to support a mission for the homeless down on Hill Street. Evelyn cheerfully cares for her psychotic mother and three aging and ill-tempered aunts.

"But statistically they don't amount to a hill of beans," I argued.

Numbers have no charm for Abigail. "On the average, we all grow older every day," was her reply, "and a bean-hill hides more beans than you'd think." She takes after her paternal grandmother in her indifference to things measured and analyzed. And she's very feminine—a slim lady with soft curves and an artless nature. But she's more complicated than she looks, and in La Aldea it was, in the end, her insight more than my engineering sense that uncovered the mystery, spotted the villain, and made two people very happy.

She was sitting close to me, as she always does when we're out driving, and put her head on my shoulder. It's a gesture that never fails to make me feel both tender and protective—though heaven knows Abigail can take care of herself. After a minute she said, "Irish is nice, but I like El Dorado better. What's he like?"

We were passing through typical Southern California hills, golden with wild oats in the morning sun, and she always has preferred them to the mixed greens of the East.

She was born and grew up in verdant Philadelphia, but we met thirty-five years ago when she was working her curious magic along the coast northwest of Los Angeles. Her question was about business.

"I've only talked to him on the phone. He sounded interesting. Invited us to dinner tonight."

"Sultan hires the Wizard blind?" Usually you meet a client and discuss the problem before you get his business.

"Bud Williams recommended me. And it's really a simple job. They want to let their computers send numbers over the telephone." I don't really need to take such jobs. Over the years, working with computers and consulting, I'd made enough money to retire and play golf. But I'm not a golfer, and love my work.

"What will they say to each other, your innocent machines?" she asked. "Ah. Here comes the town." There were trees and buildings ahead in a wide valley, and we read the signs: The Town Café: home cooking; Harkness Nursery, fruit and shade trees; Davidson Motel, color TV, pool, air-conditioned; Aldea Estates, Homes from $79,950; The Cloisters, luncheon and dinner; Rotary Club Tuesday noon; La Aldea City limits, elevation 950 feet, population 5700. "What's the use of counting souls? She asked. "Might as well count clouds, or breakers at the beach."

"It helps the tax man collect his money," I replied, "and tells the salesman and the politician where to pay attention." I looked at my watch. "We're a little early. How about a cup of coffee at the Town Café?"

"Coffee and gossip," she said, nodding.

By now we were driving down the residential part of Main Street, with sprawling, low-slung stucco houses set back from the road. The cross streets were flower names: Buttercup, Camellia, Daffodil, Edelweiss, Fuchsia . . . I must have missed Aster. I guessed the streets parallel to Main would the First, Second, Third, and Fourth, and later discovered I was right. Finally we came to the business district—sidewalks and slant-in parking. The café was at Marigold, the only corner in town with a stop light, next to the bank: a prime location. We parked and went in. It was a typical small café, white walls and a linoleum floor. There were eight tables on the right and a counter on the left with stools where you could buy candy or a milk shake or a cup of coffee, or have something to eat while you read the newspaper.

The waitress broke off her conversation with three men at a table by the window. "Good mornin'," she said, and seated us. "Coffee?" She was carrying a thermos.

"Yes," I replied. "And cream and sugar."

"You've a lovely town here," said Abigail. "I hadn't expected we'd bundle into such a sweet, small place so near to LA."

The waitress poured, and smiled. "We're the best-kept secret in two counties," she said. "Used to be nobody wanted to live here 'cause the TV reception was so bad. The hills block us off, you know. Now we got Cable, but a lot of us 'ud rather read or visit than watch. Back in a minute." She went to the counter, where a boy was serving an omelet to a tired-looking man in dirty coveralls, and returned with a small pitcher she had filled with real cream. She was blond and middle-aged, with blue eyes and a figure tending towards but not yet achieving fat. A badge on her yellow uniform named her Sadie.

"We saw the sign for those Aldes Estates outside town," I said. "Won't they change things—bring In a lot of new people?"

"You'll have to ask Tom Valley over there," Sadie replied, motioning toward the front table. "He's sellin' 'em.

He's the old gentleman." Mr. Valley had white hair, and wore a blue suit and a distinguished look. His companions were listening as he explained something. One had a white coat, and I figured him to be the local pharmacist. As we watched, the door opened and a man in work clothes came in and joined them. "Excuse me," said Sadie, and she took the newcomer a cup and filled it with coffee. The four men talked with her for a minute, and then she returned.

"Can I bring you anything else?" she asked.

"Just keep our cups full," Abigail said. "I'll bet that front table's the town's meetinghouse, and every day Mr. Valley and his chums stop by for full cups and conversation. What's the latest news, Sadie?"

"Nothin' much," she said, and then went on to contradict herself. "They arrested Jack Abricot again last night 'cause of the language he was usin' out at the tavern, but they should leave him be—he watches his tongue when there are outsiders around. And old Mrs. Wanger called the mayor to complain about that big hole in the road by her house. Not that she drives, just she's the kind of lady always lookin' out for her neighbors. And the school board is arguin' what to do about Miss Able, she's a teacher shares her house with Archie Whitmore. Trouble is, she's a little too happy about livin' in sin. And of course the whole town is takin' sides on the Hooper union." Evidently Sadie was a critical node in the town's rumor, report, and romance network.

"What's the Hooper union?" I asked.

"Ed Hooper was born here, and started up this company four years ago. Real modern electronics business. Now the union wants to organize him, and he's been fightin' it."

"Hooper Electronics?" I asked. They built a very successful computer plotter, but I hadn't realized they were located in La Aldea.

"That's right. He treats his folks fine, but the union says he should treat 'em better. What are you folks doin' in town? Thinkin' of settlin' here?"

"No," I replied. "We're here on business." It was clear that whatever we told Sadie would be passed around town in ten minutes, and I didn't know what my client would think about that.

Abigail wasn't so reticent. "Emil is going to get Mr. Bowman's newspaper computers talking so they can tell each other fables. I'm along to explain the fables to Emil, who's just an engineer and doesn't understand such things. Is Mr. Bowman a man to appreciate story-telling?"

"Bill Bowman's another native, and yes he likes a good story. He's always laughin' and cheerful. That's his son David, workin' the counter."

David was the boy we had noticed before. He must have been about eighteen, was dark-haired and handsome, but wasn't smiling. Apparently he hadn't inherited his father's enthusiasm for life. I looked at my watch. "We'd better be going. My appointment's in fifteen minutes. May we have the bill?"

Sadie wrote it out, and while I fished for change explained how to get to the offices of the *Weekly Aldean*. Ten minutes later we pulled up in front of a two-story brick building, and climbed the stairs to find ourselves in an open room where four people were working at computer keyboards. Two windows looked out on the street in front and a couple more probably gave a view of the alley behind. The room was painted a dull gray. A very pretty young woman got up to greet us. She had dark hair framing a heart-shaped face.

"You must be the Limes," she said. "I'm Caroline Bowman. Bill is expecting you." We shook hands, and she led us to an office marked "W. Bowman, Editor and Publisher". She knocked, and opened the door to a baritone "come in."

Bowman was a stout man, compact and sturdy, his posture a little stiff. He was coatless, and wore his sleeves rolled up, displaying muscular, suntanned, hairy arms. A fringe of graying hair circled his bald head. His office was full of books and photographs, and looked out on Primrose Street. A personal computer stood on a table against the wall next to a big old wooden desk, covered with papers. It was a scholar's room, I thought.

"Good morning," Bowman said, coming around the desk to shake hands. I introduced him to Abigail, and explained that she traveled with me on consulting trips, now the children were grown. "An excellent arrangement," he said. "I try to take Caroline with me when I travel, too." So she must be his wife. She was young enough to be a daughter, and far too young to be David's mother. "Sit down, sit down. Would you like some tea or coffee?"

We explained we had stopped at the café on the way to his office, and had seen his son "I had hoped to get David working here at the paper this summer," he said, a little wistfully, "but he didn't want to. It's hard, sometimes, for a son to work for a father who has created something. I think David thinks he stands in a shadow, and is afraid his father'll be disappointed if he just plumbs or clerks for a living."

"I don't think you need to worry," Caroline said. "David'll turn out just fine."

"And it depends on the boy, and the father," Abigail put in. "Fathers are like airports or railway stations. One boy will see his as the terminal you reach after a lifetime's journey, while the next regards his as the boarding point for the trip of a lifetime—where he kills Goliath, or builds the tallest skyscraper, or hews a Venus out of marble. And some fathers don't care whether their children grow up to use a screwdriver or a scalpel, as long as they use it with delight."

Bowman laughed. "I'm a father who doesn't insist on the scalpel," he said, "but I don't think David regards me as either a starting point or a destination. He thinks of me as the old bus depot, going to seed in the bad end of town, and wishes I were Cape Canaveral, where the rockets take off for the moon and beyond. But maybe we'd better get down to business. Are you going to sit in on this dreary computer talk, Abigail?"

"I always like to hear the front part, before the trees overgrow the forest," said Abigail. "Then I know what Emil's trying to do."

"It should be an easy job," Bowman said. "As I explained on the phone, Emil, we've got five ATE personal computers that the reporters and Caroline and I use to write stories, and a CIC minicomputer that lays out the pages and prepares tapes for the typesetting equipment—and does our bookkeeping and so on. We used to move copy from the PCs to the mini by hand; the reporters dumped their stories onto diskettes from their computers, and carried the disks to the mini room where they were read into the make-up program.

"We've known there were changes we could make so we could send stories between computers directly, without having to use the diskettes, but we've always figured it just wasn't worth the trouble and expense. Then we subscribed to a new consumer news service that sends out fascinating stories on organic gardening and business rip-offs and solar energy and health foods and unusual medical techniques like acupuncture, and so on." His eyes lit up as he described these interesting topics. "The stuff comes in by wire twice a week and we wanted to be able to read it directly into the mini and then move it to the PC's so our reporters could look over the stories and edit the ones we wanted to use."

"Seems like a good plan," I said, "and entirely practical, I should think."

He nodded. "Right. So we bought the necessary electronics and programs for all the computers, and ran wires all around the offices connecting them up, and then sat back expecting miracles."

"And after you went to all this trouble, you couldn't get things to work."

"Exactly," Bowman said. "We think we followed all the instructions, and most of the transfers work sometimes, but we keep losing copy and some things just don't work at all. Our local CIC and ATE salesmen have tried to help us, but they get to arguing about who's responsible for what, or they say it's trouble with the new electronics or the programs, or with the wiring, and so finally we gave up and called on the Expert. You."

"How did you choose the particular programs and electronics you bought?" I asked. There are a lot of different ways of getting computers to talk to one another. ATE, the world's biggest computer company, and CIC, which specializes in small fast machines, each have their own patented schemes, but a dozen independent companies also offer possibilities.

"I don't have much of a mind for technical matters," Bowman replied. "I'm a journalist, not an engineer, and hardly know which end of a screwdriver is the handle. And so I left it to Virgil—that's Virgil Smith, our best and most senior reporter. He did a lot of research, and then spoke to a number of salesmen and made a choice, picking a combination that seemed less costly and more effective than either ATE's or CIC's proposals. It all looked so simple—but now, of course, we can't make it work."

"I've seen problems like this before," I said. "It'll turn out there are a dozen small things wrong, none of them very hard to find or fix. I should be able to clean everything up in a few days. But my fees are so high you'll probably wish you'd let ATE do the whole job for you."

"Perhaps, but I hate to have to depend on them. In any event, while you're here, there's one other thing we'd like you to investigate. The page layout program in the minicomputer seems to have something wrong with it; something peculiar that causes it to lose a story every few weeks. We give it four stories, say, that are to be laid out on a page, and the computer is supposed to arrange them tastefully in their columns and then divide them into lines ready to run the typesetting machine. Usually everything's works fine, but once in a while the mini will lay out only three of the four stories. I gather that the 'missing' story is still there, in the mini memory; it's just missing from the layout, where there'll be a big blank space. We can't understand what's going on."

"Likely they're stores the computer doesn't favor," Abigail said, "since everyone knows programs are partisan bigoted, just like the rest of us."

She was needling me, reminding us that programs are created by people, and people are neither impartial nor perfect. I scowled at her, and Bowman laughed. "If that's the trouble," he said, "we haven't yet been able to discern a pattern in its prejudices."

"How do you solve the problem, when it comes up?" I asked.

"We try a new layout, with the missing story in a different place," he replied. "Sometimes the new layout's unpleasing to the eye, and we have to ignore the computer's advice and set the page up by hand. It's by no means an intolerable burden, dealing with the problem on the few times it appears. But it'd be great if you could straighten it out while you're here."

"I'll have a look," I promised.

"You haven't said anything, Caroline," Abigail said. "Where's your oarlock on this ship of paper?"

Caroline actually blushed. I thought she must be even younger than she looked. "I'm Bill's girl Friday," she said. "I help with his stories and editorials, do special assignments, write some copy of my own. That sort of thing."

"She's entirely too modest," her husband said. "She is the oil that keeps the editorial machinery rolling smoothly, and she also composes a column which is one of the most popular in our newspaper."

"What's it about?" I asked.

She blushed again. "It's called Aldean Annals. Every week I write a short biography of a local resident."

"They're remarkable," Bowman said. "She always sees the useful, gracious side of the individual, no matter how irascible or unhappy or ignorant or lazy or ugly or infuriating he or she is; and even so, the story is invariably accurate. It always gives a fair picture, with the result that our readers say to themselves, 'Yep, that's just what Suzy or Hank is like,'"

Abigail is a lady whose evaluation of people is always both kind and fair, and so I noticed she looked at Caroline with new interest. "Who are you taxiderming this week?" she asked.

"Edward Hooper," she replied, "the President of a local company, and La Aldea's biggest employer."

"Thursday's issue is going to be interesting," her husband added, "for Caroline will show Hooper's good side, and in my editorial I'll be painting him as he really is." He grinned at his wife.

"That's not fair, Bill," she said, and then saw he was teasing, blushed once more. She told us, "Bill can't be tolerant when he believes injustice is being done."

"And Hooper is an unjust character?" I asked. "How's that?"

"Read the editorial on Thursday and you'll find the answer," Bowman replied, "a bolt of journalistic lightning of the kind I fling, in every issue, at the wicked and the foolish. Next week I shall harass the school board, whose members are about to torment poor little Miss Able, just because she's in love. You'd think we were still living in the Middle Ages."

"Sadie painted her and Mr. Whitmore for us when we were at the café this morning," Abigail said. "Is it True Love, Caroline?"

"Jennifer is a sweet and honest lady and a good teacher. Archie . . . ." again there was that lovely blush. "Archie is a different kind of person."

"Archie," Bowman said, "is charming, intelligent, lazy, broke, and permanently unemployed. He's a typical product of America's inequitable society, and there are those who say he is taking advantage of our once-virginal schoolteacher. But let's return to our original subject. How do you propose to proceed in assaulting our problem, Emil?"

"First I'll spend some time studying the manuals that cover your equipment and programs. Then this afternoon

I'd like someone to show me just what the problems are. Who's the best person for that?"

"All of us know something about it," Bowman said, "but your best informant will be Virgil, since he chose the equipment and programs and is more knowledgeable about the system than anyone else. And of course he's been trying to cure all the problems, himself. Caroline, will you introduce him to Emil, and ask him to assemble the manuals and find a suitable place for Emil to work? I've got some things I have to do."

"All right, Bill. Will you be joining us for lunch?"

"No, I believe I'll just have a sandwich at my desk"

"Abigail," I said, "if you wouldn't mind being on your own, I'd like to eat my lunch over the manuals."

"Suits me just fine," Abigail replied. "Give me time to go out and wander roam the town." Bowman reminded us we'd be having dinner at their home at seven, and gave us the address, and Caroline took us back into the bull pen. She introduced us to Virgil and the rest of the staff, explaining what it was I needed. Virg looked to be in his early thirties, taller than Bowman and Caroline, sort of undistinguished-looking, with brown hair and horned-rimmed glasses. But he was clearly glad to have some help, and he led me off to the manuals while Abigail started getting acquainted with the others.

CHAPTER 2

Monday morning and afternoon

It was a big, ugly, turbid room after the peace and distance of Bill's office. Emil went off with Virgil looking wistful because he was having to leave Caroline. She pretended not to notice, and we talked to the two folks who remained: Sally Jensen, a part-time reporter looking earnest troubled and a hesitant smile; and George Rawlins, the paper's photographer. Sally right away off back to work, but George, short and balding no necktie wanted something.

"Your damn computers can write the copy," said he to me, very belligerent, "but they can't take the pictures. Copy is easy, just one letter after another. Pictures is the whole thing at once, at a glance." A slight man he was, a two-pack-a-day man, with worry lines and dents in his forehead and no one to go home to at night.

Caroline tried to fend him off. "Oh please, George . . . ." She began, but I interrupted.

"Computers can't even write the copy," said I. "They don't have enough pity and humor and sympathy and indignation and charity, and maybe you don't have enough of those things to take good pictures so show me some, and I'll see."

He looked surprised. "You've got a nerve," said he. "Uppity and bad-tempered, just like every dame I've ever known. But come on. I'll show you." He led me to a file cabinet at one end of the room. Caroline followed, distressed she was, but he pulled out a folio and handed it to me, then leaned against the wall, arms folded, smirking a little, and watched.

I spread the pictures out on a table and saw right away: George knew how to do it. A small boy looking up wondering fiercely if someone was going to give him something he had to have. A view of a lost, lonesome, weary La Aldea from the hills behind town. A pretty woman, her shoulders hitched, hands in her coat pockets, staring worried into the distance or the future. An old house in the country, in the rain, hoping the next year would be better. A young girl maybe twelve, her hand on her father's arm adoring him with eyes that would see faults and failures in another two or three years but which now knew he was wise and good. A fence holding back the world from a house behind.

I looked up from the pictures. "Could I have one, George?" I asked.

He shrugged. "Help yourself."

I picked out a Main Street in the summer sun full of ice cream cones and cotton dresses and barefoot kids and cars with the tops down, seeming cheerful until you saw the tired and anxious old man almost hidden in the crowd. "Thank you," said I. There'll never be a computer that touches the likes of you. What're you taking today?"

"Whatever catches the eye. And crabby Helen Abernathy, next week's Aldean Annal."

"He'll drive me over to see her," said Caroline. "He takes the pictures while I do the interview."

"Who is Ms Abernathy and how do you choose?"

"People make suggestions, and I keep my eyes and ears open. Helen was the town Clerk for more than forty years.

She's going on ninety now, but she knew the town when it was small. She remembers the parents and grandparents of a lot of today's citizens. She knows Bill's folks, for example."

"And my mother, too," said George. "The two of 'em used to give me holy hell. Told me I was growing up wild. Agreed I'd never amount to anything." He gave us another smirk. "Maybe I'll get even, with a picture that'll show her the way she really is—long in the tooth and short in the temper."

While we talked a lanky, gawky man in shirtsleeves and vest came up the stairs faltered across to us. "Caroline," said he, "could you assist me for a moment or two?"

"Certainly, Martin. Abigail, this is Martin Nears, our accountant. Martin, Abigail's husband is fixing our computer problems. What's the trouble?" He had the perplexed look of a lost child who's drifted away from his parents in a big zoo, half-afraid half fascinated by the lions, and wondering if the turtles are as old as they say, and whether the storks bring the babies.

"I'm unable to achieve a balance at the moment, Caroline, and you seem always able to determine where I've gone astray."

She made a face, but before she went downstairs with Martin, we talked agreed we'd meet at Sadie's Café for lunch.

"Hard to imagine a bookkeeper who can't add, ain't it?" said George when they were gone. "I can't figure if he's dumb, or just likes beauty with him at the ledgers."

"After thirty years you ought to know," I told him. On Bowman's office wall next to the big yacht picture sailing a brisk wind, there'd been a smaller one showing Bill and George and Martin holding up what looked was the first edition of the *Weekly Aldean*, all bright and new the young men and paper both.

George regarded me suspicious, but decided Bill had told me. "Maybe I ought, and maybe I oughtn't," he replied. "Right from the first Bill had to lead him by the hand, or nose. And now Martin drives a Cadillac, and he and his wife live up on the hill. Says he invested in the stock market. You tell me: is it dumb luck, or does he just hide a head for figures?"

"There's smarts and luck, both, in 'most everything," said I. "Even in pictures."

"Sure." He pointed to the one he'd given me, of summer cold and hot on Main Street. "That kid and the cute couple and the old car and the worried gaffer just happened by at the right time and were in the right place. Bill and Martin and I just happened to be available when a newspaper was wanted. But they've got ahead, and I still live in the flatlands, poor as a church mouse." He shrugged, looked at his watch. "I gotta go load some cameras. You gonna be all right?" I said yes I had to find a place to live, and he went away leaving me thinking why church mice had to be poor these days of generous congregations and whether he was, with pictures people would delight to buy.

Starting out I saw Sally frowning at her keyboard. She seemed about 35 a round face no wrinkles yet, in a very plain dress with flowers. I stopped to visit wondering. "Are you writing of earthquakes and accidents?" said I.

She looked up surprised smiling a little. "No. It's an article about the local farms. But what made you think disasters?"

"Your face is long like Bill Cosby Huxtable worrying about daughter Vanessa."

The smile grew shyly a little more. "I didn't know it showed so. Trouble is, the story is taking much longer than I figured it would. I'd hoped for another assignment this week, and now there won't be time."

"Won't there be enough to fill the paper?" asked I.

"That's not it. It's just that I need . . . We stringers are paid by the story, not by the hour or the column-inch, and I had counted on a bigger paycheck this week."

"Maybe sometimes stories take less time than you guess so it washes in the long run?"

"Not often. But it's my own fault—Mr. Bowman and I agreed how long it should take. Anyway, I have another job, so I'll be all right."

"What do you do when you're not stringing?"

"I wait on tables, evenings, at a bar out in the Oaks. It's not too bad, and sometimes the tips are fabulous."

When you say it's not too bad it is, and I bet some rough customers and a lewd boss hardly made up for fabulous tips in the eye of a nice girl who wanted to write not flirt.

I didn't keep her from her from her work much longer and downstairs back into the sun I drove the car to Main Street. The Davidson Motel was near the edge of town at the corner of Sunflower, frayed rug in a lobby needing paint. Evan Jitney the proprietor at the front desk had our reservation and checked me in and was as talkative as Sadie, so I heard some more news. The mayor was putting on weight, consequent to having given up smoking. His Task Force was bogged down and couldn't decide about the new school. The burglary at the Hapsworth's last week must have been done by someone from the City. Miss Able ought to kick out that Whitmore boy—he was no good at all. The town should really grow now that old man Ryan had sold off most of his property. Last winter had been extra dry, so the hills were browner than usual. Caroline Bowman's Annal last week had made everyone realize how important a good fire department is, and how lucky they were to have Elmer Wilkins as chief. The Weekly Aldean was lively, and everyone looked forward to seeing it, though Bill Bowman's opinions were outrageous—he leaned much too far in the liberal direction. Take this business about the Hooper union. Ed pays his people very well. There's never been any complaint. And then some outsider from the City comes in and tries to organize, and Bowman hears about it and insists that Hooper employees will never get a fair shake unless they have a union. Hogwash, was Mr. Jitney's opinion. All the unions do is featherbed, and make it hard for you to get rid of the incompetents. And Bowman was stirring up hard feelings in his own family, because everyone knew that young David Bowman was sweet on Ed Hooper's daughter Elizabeth. David lived with his mother, who had worked as secretary for a lawyer in Woodland Hills since she and Bill were divorced. A pity, that. She's a fine woman, and everybody'd thought they'd been very happy.

Got the key to our room it a bit dingy, the bed with a sagging middle let me put our bags there and I unpacked a little and went browsing walking. After Sunflower came Zinnia and probably they used it instead of Tulip so's to make the town seem bigger. Just weeds beyond so I turned looking while I moseyed back. Frame house with two girls talking on the porch in a swing chair. Bald barber leaning against the door of his empty shop, nodded hello. Big red dog loping sheepishly alongside a nervy trotting fox terrier. Methodist Church with sprinklers watering the lawn parking had a handicapped space. Row of sparrows on a telephone line. Two blocks of dignified houses, communing together in the shade on their fortune and the town's. Supermarket, open seven am to eleven pm seven days a week, shopping carts in the parking lot. Cal's gas station used tires, careful repairs and a special lube job.

The next block a dime store, shoe store, dry cleaner, photo shop, florist, jeweler, ladies' wear and the drug store on the corner. I bought a pencil, tried on boots, asked how long to clean a sweater, looked at cameras, smelled the flowers, priced pearl necklaces, and got some toothpaste, and everybody was as friendly as churches on Easter Sunday. The florist slim neat had grown an eight-pound zucchini at home, thought the fire chief was underpaid. Girl in the dime store said David Bowman was dreamy, awful how he was so stuck on that icky Hooper girl. George Rawlins sold his photos at an art gallery somewhere in LA, so said the camera man whose wife liked working on the assembly line at Hooper Electronics. Dry clean lady thought Miss Able had a right to live however she wanted and that Mr. Hooper ought to be ashamed of himself denying his people the right to join the Union. Virg Smith and the shoe clerk often were crew on Bill Bowman's thirty-foot sailboat, surprising how much help Bill needed, and young David didn't like to sail much and Caroline was just a beginner. Jeweler wondered if he ought to put in a burglar alarm, told me Ellen Neare had bought a necklace just like that one last month. Pharmacist said Fred O'Leary the police chief was arguing with the mayor about night patrols in town.

In Ladies' Wear I asked a green sweater the clerk bright-looking showed me one. I thanked her no found her name Alice Brightsmith and said I'd visited the newspaper.

"Did you meet the Bowmans, Bill and Caroline?" she asked.

"And Virg Smith and George Rawlins and Martin Neare and Sally Jensen," said I.

"All nice folks. Caroline doesn't spend as much on clothes as she should, a pretty girl like her. Says she has a limited budget. Mrs. Neare, on the other hand, can spend what she wants."

"Husbands sometimes put chains on purses that should have strings," said I.

"I guess Bill Bowman uses a chain, then. But he's a charming guy. My husband and I see him at the Chamber of Commerce"

"George Rawlins has great pictures instead of charm."

Alice laughed. "Aren't they super? Don't know why he lives in this small town. He sells pictures in L.A. and New York. Should move there."

I agreed he should but should doesn't always mean would. Thanked her and on my way.

La Aldea was all connected to itself, with not much outside coming in, and you heard what everybody thought about the news, which wasn't Prince Charles or Senator Kennedy or Wall Street or Arabs, it was what the neighbors were doing. Some folks are curious about next door so they can help out by bringing a cake or minding the kids, and some sour like to complain criticize so they don't have to examine their own consciences or because they have done and didn't like it.

Caroline was at the café early when I got there, and introduced me to David busy at tables and to his girl Elizabeth Hooper having a soda at the counter. Sadie showed us a table in the corner, and Caroline asked how I'd spent the morning and I told her she had a friendly town and wondered how long she'd lived here.

"Bill hired me about six years ago, right out of school. I'd majored in journalism in college—started writing stories when I was a small girl, and my father read me Aesop's Fables. Mrs. Pauma had been getting out the Annals for over twenty hears, but she was retiring and Bill wanted me to take over. Virgil and George helped, and I caught on pretty quick, though of course I pitch in with other things, too. We all have to—it's such a small paper." She looked at the menu. "We'd better order. I don't want to be late over at Mrs. Abernathy's."

We picked out soups and sandwiches and after a while with some talk and some silence and some help she got around to telling about Bill and love and weddings.

"Mrs. Bowman was working at the paper when I came, but they weren't getting on. In a while they separated. I don't really know what the problem was. Bill never talked about it, and the divorce was quiet and as they say amicable. Once he moved out of their house, he started dating me."

"But you'd been dating other people, like Virgil, before then," said I, so she blushed like she did when anyone said anything close to the heart or bone.

"Yes. I was invited out by various people, including Virgil. Even George took me to dinner once. But Bill is so . . . so impressive, and brilliant. When I saw he was interested in me, I was just very flattered."

"Love and flattery are two things."

"Of course. But it's nice to be admired by somebody admirable; and over the months, as I got to know him, it was easy to fall in love."

"Months is a long time," said I. With Emil and me it had been immediate love, though he didn't see it until after I smooched him a kiss. Sometimes he's slow to find what's under his nose, even though or maybe because he believes he's a logical thinker with problems defined and data piled up and his hypotheses formulated and tested like any Newton.

Another blush acknowledging the long time. "We weren't in any hurry. We saw each other every day." She couldn't be cold-blooded, not with all that quick color, but she sounded as if love settled over you like a wet night fog rather than kindling igniting you like a torch in tinder country. "We were married in '84."

Lunch came, and we talked about La Aldean folks and doings until George arrived to take her away to her interview. David and Elizabeth were still talking between his serving out lunches, so I took my coffee over where they pretended they wouldn't mind if I joined on.

"David says your husband's a computer expert," said Elizabeth. Across the counter when he had time David was holding her hand so everyone would know they were together. She had freckles and wore braids which made her look about fourteen, but her figure and poise and the dime store job all said seventeen or more.

"That's what he tells me and his customers. And I've seen him unravel a lot of knotty and tangled skeins with computers in the middle, so I'm inclined to think he's right. He's not always right, though . . . Haven't you found men often wrong, Elizabeth?"

"It's funny you should ask that, Mrs. Lime. I've just been trying to persuade David he shouldn't be so hard on his father.

"*He's* not right, 'Liz," said David. "Who is he to say whether your dad should fight the union? He's just poking his nose into something he doesn't know anything about. He doesn't want to be fair. Why doesn't he stick to writing stories on Rotary club meetings, and traffic accidents?" You could see David didn't know yet how hard it is to make choices so was thinking his father hadn't been fair to his mother or to him. Bill thought his son was shy of father's fame and didn't see the hurt from being abandoned.

"You're saying what you feel, just like everyone has to," I told him, "and the editorials are where your father can say what he feels. Sometimes he's right and sometimes not and the people who read them know that, so don't worry."

"Hardly anyone hears, when I say what I feel. His opinions are in print where everyone has to read them."

"But like Mrs. Lime says, David, he has a right to his opinion. And he publishes letters from people who disagree with him."

Just then Virgil Smith came into the cafe with a worry look and asked David to step outside for a minute they went on the sidewalk just out the door. "You're doing just the right thing, Elizabeth," said I. "Don't let him get too far away from his father." David wasn't liking what Virgil was telling, but Virgil didn't like it either and I knew when they told us Elizabeth would like it least of all. David came back in and said something to Sadie, then took his apron off and Elizabeth by the arm.

"Come on 'Liz," said he. "I want to talk to you for a minute," and they went out very fast.

"Who's hurt her?" said I to an angry Virgil looking after the two of them . . .

"What?" The train of thought was interrupted and he saw I was there. "Oh. Her father has. We just heard, at the office. He's in the hospital, in what they call 'serious but not critical' condition. The police have arrested an irate husband in Hidden Hills who caught him in bed with his wife and beat the hell out of him. The LA papers have the story."

"How likely is it true?" I asked.

"Bill called the police to check, and there doesn't seem to be any doubt. The description fits, and his driver's license was in his clothes, and the woman knew him by his own name. At Hooper's office they say he went out to lunch early, as he does every Monday. The local police told Mrs. Hooper, but when we called her at home, there was no answer."

Outside the door I looked they weren't in sight. At the next street and around the corner in a hurry where the sign pointed the City Park, and there I found them sitting close a bench in the shade of a poplar tree. She was crying disbelieving with his arm around her. I sat on a bench across the path and looked somewhere else, tears on my own cheeks. No way to know why Hooper was hurting all these people. Maybe proving he's male, maybe no love at home, maybe hot pants?

David held her his handkerchief with the other hand and she blew her nose and after a while said to me.

"David says it may not be true, Mrs. Lime," Said she. "It just can't be. Why would father . . . ." she held out her hand to me and I joined them and borrowed the handkerchief for my own tears.

"That's right," said I. "They may be mixed up and you should find out soon but it may be true, I don't know. Remember David's father is wrong sometimes in the paper, and your father may have made a mistake too."

"How can we find out? What should I do?"

"Why don't we visit your father, at the hospital?" Said David.

"That's a good idea, Elizabeth," said I. "But you also have to think about your mother, for she'll need you and you her. Have David take you home first and if she's not there phone around and try to find her at the hospital or a relative's or wherever you think. When you find her, stick with her, but if you don't, leave her a note saying where you are and then go see your father."

She hadn't thought about her mother and for a moment she looked both sad and perplexed and told us, "Poor Mother. She won't know which way to turn. You're right. The first thing to do is to find her." She wiped away a few more tears then got up, taking David's arm but for comfort not support and said, "Thank you, Mrs. Lime. Could you tell us where you're staying? And would you mind if I called you, if . . . ."

I told her the Davidson and that I didn't mind, and they hurried away while I wandered another part of Main Street. At the book store and the sweet shop and the tobacconist and the milliner and the gift shop and the ski and tennis place and the other shoe shop they were hearing about the Hooper scandal. The news came on quick phone calls received with surprised eyebrows, or from hurried visits by folks on their way to somewhere else. It passed like a breeze ruffling a quiet lake, and the little waves scrabbled and pushed along before they died out. It was a pity and serves him right and poor Mrs. Hooper and who would have guessed and I always wondered and his wife is such a flibbertigibbet. The town was taking sides like Lizzie Borden. Ed Hooper was too proud for his own good and certainly paid attention to the ladies, and his wife talked too much and played a terrible game of bridge but was faithful and as loving as anyone could expect, and Elizabeth was a spoiled only child too attached to her father so it would be hard on her.

Back at the Café late in the afternoon Sadie told me the Hoopers were no different from anyone else in town. She didn't mean adultery and scatterbrains and I figured she was right whether she meant Aldea or everywhere in the world where we all bring troubles on ourselves.

CHAPTER 3

Monday afternoon

It's fun, tackling a new job. There's always some kind of challenge that'll sharpen your wit and stimulate your inventiveness. The consultant is generally called in only when there's an emergency. Either something has to be done in a hurry and your customer hasn't time to learn how to do it, or there's some sort of sticky problem no one has been able to solve. The 'hurry' clients have usually promised something they can't deliver. I remember one—a manufacturer—who'd told the world his new printer would be ready in six months, though his premier designer had just quit and his engineering group was in turmoil. When you take on a 'hurry' job, you have to figure on working seven-day weeks and twelve-hour days. It's tiring, but it pays well.

The 'problem' clients are more fun. They require less stamina, and more brains. Often you're called in as a last resort, when all sorts of bright people have broken their lances, gone down in flames, fallen on their noses, laid eggs, fizzled out and sunk to the bottom of the sea without a trace. You have to succeed where others have missed the boat. Often the client is in a panic.

Bill Bowman wasn't in a panic, but he had a problem, and I've developed a routine for jobs like his. The first step is always to listen to people tell you how things are supposed to work and how they're actually working, and the second is to read the manuals that tell how things were *designed* to work. It's surprising how often folks buy the wrong program or equipment for the job they want done—like buying a snowplow in November, and being disappointed you can't use it to mow the lawn in July. The mistakes are generally the result of wishful thinking rather than foolishness or stupidity. When the salesman—or for that matter the preacher or the doctor or the neighbor or the uncle or the boss—talks, we hear what we want to hear, rather than what was said.

My conversation with Bowman was part of step one, but had been disappointing. He hadn't really known much about his troubles, steering me to Virg as the expert who would fill me in on the details. I was hungry, so I skipped to step two, and sat in a small, quiet room reading manuals while I ate lunch. The sandwich wasn't bad, washed down with milk, though the whole-wheat bread I had asked for was pretty flabby. The manuals were just what one would expect—a mixed bag of clear exposition, sloppy improvisation, and fuzzy orientalese like 'press momentarily the button F9 to try first the working'. Some of them I had seen before, on other jobs; the others I read through and understood, more or less. Later, when I began to see better what the problems were, I would know where to look in the manuals. At first glance, it appeared that Virg hadn't bought a snowplow to mow the lawn: the stuff he'd picked out should do the job he wanted done.

Once I understood how everything was *supposed* to work, I found Virg and asked for a demonstration of his troubles. He was impressively familiar with the system, and sat me down next to his desk so he could show me all the features on his own PC. I was beginning to like him. I'm prejudiced in favor of anyone who's taken a lot of trouble to learn something about computers.

"Right," he started out. "It's pretty confusing, I'm afraid. There are five PC'S, you remember. There's Bill's, mine, and Caroline's. And then two others used by Sally and the part-timers. Actually, there are still another two downstairs. But they're used by the circulation and advertising people. They don't have the communications connection, so we don't have to worry about them. Then there's the CIC mini, also down below near the accountants and the press room. The mini is the only machine connected to the outside. It's supposed to take in the new wire service stories Monday and Wednesday mornings.

"There are four general problems. The two worst are trouble sending stuff between the PC's, and trouble on transfers between PC's and the mini. Caroline's PC, for example, is a basket case. She can't talk to any other PC. And transfers between my PC and Sally's are occasionally bad.

"Another problem is I myself sometimes can't use my word processor to update a document. And finally, the mini sometimes has trouble laying out pages so they'll look good in print."

"Bill told me about that problem," I said.

"The whole thing's a mess," Virg said. "Reminds me of the first car I ever owned, in college—an old, yellow Chevy—supposed to be racy, but in fact kept stopping at bad times. What's worst of all is that everything seems to go to pieces when we're busiest, and desperately need for everything to work right."

"Give me a demonstration. How do you send or receive stuff on your own PC to and from the mini?"

Virgil turned to his keyboard. For the next hour he showed me his problems,

"Okay," I said, when he'd finished. "I think I get the picture. Will it be all right if I take over the mini for a while? And can I use the spare PC? I'd like to move it downstairs with the mini to do some tests."

Virgil said I could do what I liked and to let him know when the mini was available again. We went back upstairs, and he helped me move the spare PC and my tool case down to the mini room. Then he excused himself, and I went to work earning my fee. It was just the kind of job I liked: a clear-cut problem likely to yield to a calm, patient, rational analysis. Whenever I tackle something like this I remember my father's pride when I repaired the family doorbell years ago. I was twelve and had just read a library book on electricity, and I suppose it was that first unlikely success—after a little poking around, I had found a loose screw somewhere—that led me finally into engineering.

The minicomputer was a bunch of chassis mounted in a big frame about as tall as I am and maybe three feet wide, with lights flashing on a front panel. I went to work. That afternoon I found and repaired a bad circuit in the mini, and learned a lot more about the layout problem. Virgil said a company called Programming Journalists Associated. PJA had provided the layout program. He had written to them as soon as he figured out what was happening, but they weren't any help at all.

While he told me this he had made another request on his PC, and it had gone to work on something.

"What are you doing now?" I asked.

"Oh, it's a spare-time exercise in futile curiosity. Last year there was a story on one of the wire services about a body—a skeleton, I should say—they found over in

Arizona. No one knew who it was. But nearby they found an unusual gold ring with a raindrop design on it. Thing is, I vaguely remember we published a story some years ago about a ring like that. Don't remember the details, and no one else remembers the story at all. I tried to find it by having the PC search through all the old issues looking either for the word 'ring' or the word 'raindrop'. Didn't find the story. But maybe I made a mistake in my previous search. Or maybe the story used some other words. So now sometimes, usually evenings when I've finished a late story and don't have anything else to do, I let the PC search for not only 'ring' and 'raindrop', but also 'gold', 'jewelry', and just 'drop'."

The screen came to life, and displayed a paragraph. "Let's see what we have," Virg said. "Nope. You see. It found a rhyme by a local poet that contains the word 'raindrops'. That's not what I want." He hit a button and the PC continued its search.

"How far back do your diskette files go?" I asked.

"Back to 1981. That's when we got the computers."

"Might the story have been earlier than that?"

"Yep. It might. I'm pretty sure it wasn't more than ten years ago, but it might have been before '81. For the earlier years, we keep copies of the papers themselves, and I looked through them. It was slow work. Of course I might be misremembering."

We left the PC grinding away searching for rings.

He went back upstairs to work, and for the next couple of hours I sat, searching through old diskettes for layout errors, and trying them out on the mini as I found them. I made no progress—could see no pattern in the errors. I noticed a story missing on one of the archive diskettes I examined, but that didn't seem to have anything to do with incomplete layouts. If there was an obscure programming problem in the layout program, it was going to be tough to find. I figured I'd call the supplier tomorrow—who was it, PJA?—and make sure they hadn't solved the problem since Virgil had written his letter. If they hadn't, I'd suggest that we send PJA a sample of the trouble, and let them sort it out. That would be a lot cheaper than paying me to dig bugs out of the program.

It was nearly time to meet Abigail, so I packed up my gear and took the spare PC back upstairs. Everyone seemed to be busy, so I waved goodbye and went out to find the Davidson Motel. Abigail had been out on the town for a whole afternoon and more, and I knew she'd have made three dozen new friends, and would have that many or more lively and unusual stories to tell. She and I are as different as puppies and mountains. If the situation had been reversed, and I'd been cast ashore in La Aldea for an afternoon while she was solving someone's problem, I'd have probably wound up sitting in a library or standing in a bookshop, and wouldn't have met a soul.

CHAPTER 4

Monday Evening

Emil the dear funny man likes my red dress because it shows a lot of bosom but then he frowns when he sees Bill Bowman and Tom Valley are noticing it too. Caroline has a nicer one being newer but her outfit's more modest so she doesn't get the attention. Cynthia Valley doesn't seem to have one at all. She sees how the boys are trying to peer, though, and is laughing to herself. What is it about men and bosoms? They say fixations left over from mother's milk but it could as well be the magic of Eve's round apple or the lure of the mysterious or what their fathers taught them, which explains their devotion to baseball and next year's cars and trout fishing.

We were in the Bowman dining room the best plates and silver out. "It's the hypocrisy of it all that bothers me," Bill was saying helping himself to seconds on potatoes. "Here we have our friend Hooper, an elder in his church, a respected figure in the community, a man who insists he treats his employees in a fair and Christian manner and that a company union will only disrupt operations, and meanwhile he's carrying on a tawdry affair—marvelous word, tawdry—with a married woman whom he meets every Monday for a little fornication. It wouldn't be so bad if he hadn't been pretending to be so good."

What are we to think of men who look down the front of the dresses of their guests and still love dote on their wives I wonder, but that doesn't seem a point I can bring up.

"We shouldn't be so hard on him. Bill," said Caroline. "He's certainly desperately sorry now, himself, and wishes he had never met the woman."

A good influence is his wife but I betcha she won't deflect the course or blunt the sharpness of Thursday's editorial. Anyway my grandma taught me hypocrisy is a bad thing to disparage because so many of us are, though she was an exception I always thought.

"How is he doing?" asked Tom. "Has anyone heard?"

"As well as can be expected," said Caroline. "I called the hospital after we got home. They say he'll be there another couple of days, is all. No permanent damage."

"He was fortunate," said Bill, "but it will be interesting, now, to see how La Aldea reacts to the news. The family is of course distraught, with poor Florence not knowing whether to forgive and forget, or to bring suit, and probably settling on doing neither, but just making Hooper's life miserable for the next twenty years. Young Elizabeth will suffer more—she thinks the world of her father. And then there are the townsfolk in general. What will their response and reaction be?"

"I don't understand, Bill," said Tom Valley, helping himself to seconds. "Why should anyone respond? What is it you expect?"

"It depends. There are other philanderers in the town, and I wonder whether they'll change their ways when they see the wages of sin. Certainly there are other hypocrites—men who complain about thieves and cheat on their income tax, churchgoers who take the name of the Lord in vain, members of the Better Business Bureau who lie to their customers, Boy Scout leaders who sneak off and watch dirty movies, Sunday school teachers who don't follow the Golden Rule, secret debauchers who want Jenny Able fired. Will any of these folks note the parallel between their own behavior and Hooper's, and change their ways?"

"Not very many, I should think." said Tom. "The parallels won't be evident to the sinners themselves. In fact, most of us sinners don't even think of ourselves as sinners. We have good reasons for the bad things we're doing. If my old friend Jim Jones drives over the speed limit and hits a wall, I know it's because he was hurrying to pick up his daughter at school so it's ok."

"Well then, how about the friends and relatives of the hypocrites?" continued Bill. Words were exploding like popcorn squibs in his head, and readers would soon see all this in their weekly newspapers. "What will they do? How will they react? And what about those who have looked to Hooper for leadership—his employees, his bankers and investors? What confidence can they have in his word, when they see what a liar he's been?"

"I think the answer to that last question should put Hooper's transgressions in perspective," said Emil whose idea was going to be sensible right even with the long words. "Being a hypocrite in one realm of his life doesn't make him a liar everywhere. We're all of us frauds sometimes. I know I am." He was looking guilty but shouldn't for he's transparent like one of those little beasts you saw in your Christmas microscope when you were stuck at home on a rainy summer day. "I pretend I'll consult for anyone; but some customers I turn down because they rub me the wrong way. I tell Abigail I like her casseroles; but in fact what I really like is meat and potatoes. Just because I lie a little here and there doesn't make me a liar in all matters."

Worse than that because he says he likes all my cooking not just my casseroles and I'm a terrible cook but make it up to him in other ways. Cynthia Valley is a good cook so Emil would have a belly like Tom's if I wasn't the way I am.

"You're very generous, Emil," said Bill, "but you lean backwards too far, trying to clear Hooper. We have to distinguish the petty lies we all employ, when we tell a woman her hat is pretty, or compliment our neighbor on his daughter's new boy friend, from the kind of cruel and deceitful cheating Hooper has apparently been doing for years."

Bill was not going to see how fine the lines were so maybe a change of direction would help. "We don't want Ed Hooper's example to make everyone change his ways who pretends to be one thing but is really another," said I. "In town today Andy Archer the florist was dressed threadbare a regular Scrooge, but the stickers on his door are United Way and Red Cross. Hall Avery the shoe man complained business bad but framed certificate thanked free shoes for poor kids. And Mrs. Winthrop in the stationers scowled frowning how rude and ornery the world is, then went three blocks out of her way so I found the bookstore. And of course George Rawlins pretends he hates women but doesn't at all."

"Walt a minute now, Abigail," said Bill. "A hypocrite is a fellow who puts on virtues he doesn't have, so people who put on vices they don't have must be something else." Then he looked worried thoughtful. "Or maybe are they hypocrites too? It's a good question. I shall have to consult the dictionary." The word man unmanned or maybe unworded and it's good for him.

"Why are you so sure George doesn't despise women?" asked Cynthia. "I've never doubted his misogyny."

"His pictures of us worried or loving or human otherwise deny all the bitter scoffing words," said I, "and today for example he fretted how I would spend my afternoon." And he had tried to court Caroline, but who wouldn't?

"Anyway, she's right about Andy and Hall and Winnie," said Tom. "Let's hope they don't change."

"How did you come to meet them, Abigail?" said Cynthia.

"Oh, I was just wandering meandering like a tumbleweed in the March winds," and I told them the look of the town all clean neat and the warmth of the folks and some of what they said. "There was young Sammy Valdez I met too who sails with you folks in the Cal-35 in the picture on your office wall I suppose."

Bill looked a cheerful puppy seeing the evening leash brought out. "That's right," said he. "Our boat's the Faraway, and we keep her at the marina at Oxnard, and venture out whenever we can, usually Fridays, since the paper's put to bed early Thursday. Caroline's becoming a most proficient sailor."

"You spent this last weekend out at the islands, didn't you?" said Tom.

"Yes. Yes, indeed. We were at San Miguel, where the weather was perfect and we caught a fifteen-pound halibut."

"That'd just about pay your marina fees for the month," said Emil.

Bill laughed. "Not quite," said he, "but it surely was good eating, and we still have some left. In the freezer."

"Been sailing long?" said I.

"Since I was a kid. Summers in high school I used to hitchhike up to Santa Barbara and hang around the harbor hoping someone would ask me to crew for them, or to work on their boats. Those were the days before fiberglass hulls and aluminum masts, of course, and there was always a lot of scraping and painting and varnishing to do."

"You were an unusual kid if you liked scraping and painting," said Tom.

"I suppose so. I'm not much good with my hands, but the nasty jobs often led to more interesting ones. Several times I was crew on trips to Frisco, and on one occasion I got to Mexico." His eyes lit like looking at visions in the distance. "That was a memorable trip."

"I what way?" said Emil.

"I'd almost forgotten about it. The boat's owner was a wealthy lawyer. I thought him ancient, though I suppose he was in his forties. And he was accompanied by his wife. She was a beautiful woman, and I fell in love with her. I don't imagine she ever really noticed I was present. She had a figure like Caroline's, and always wore a two-piece bathing suit, and when we entered the harbor on our return, I contrived to steal the top to that suit. Kept it in my room at home for months. I don't know whatever became of it."

"Romantic thievery," said Cynthia.

"You're right." said Bill. "Absolutely right. I was a lovelorn cutpurse. But it was a romantic trip, sailing south in the summer."

"The nights on the water are lovely," said Caroline, who'd blushed when her figure was complimented, wanted a new subject. "Glorious stars, and the phosphorescence, and the boat rocking gently, and the water slapping against the hull." She got up and started to clear the plates, ready to bring in dessert, and I helped her.

"Distant islands pulling you, the home harbor pushing, heeling 'way over afraid you'll tip", I put in.

"And the salt smell, and the snap of the halyards on the mast, and the lights and voices from the boat moored next to us, and the rush of the water across the stones on the beach, and the occasional splash of a fish escaping a bigger one." Bill was a romantic about his boat as well, and Caroline had learned, though maybe she hadn't yet been out afraid in a big storm like Emil and I when the kids were small.

Sailing and the ocean we talked for the next half hour with our dessert lemon cake, then left the table for coffee in the neatly furnished living room sofa chairs coffee table and Emil asked about La Aldea.

"How is it that the town hasn't grown more?" said he. "Sadie said it was because TV reception wasn't good, but that's pretty hard to believe. This'd be a great place to live if you worked in the west Valley, or even over the hill in Santa Monica or Westwood."

"It's easily explained," answered Tom. "Most of the land around the city, between us and the National Forest to the south, and between us and the freeway on the north, belonged to Charlie Ryan. Until he began to sell out, there was just no room to expand." Talking real estate he was the excited impresario with eyes lit up, just found a lost play by Oscar Wilde. For the first time we saw him a young man before his grey baldness.

"And now developers have moved in," said Bill, "and the city's in the throes of change. It's a tragedy, really, with the La Aldean Estates selling fast, and other building projects under way. In the coming few years the city will double in size, and then double again, and nothing can be done—the town couldn't afford to buy Ryan's land for parks or green space, even if that's what we citizens wanted."

"How come this fellow Ryan didn't sell earlier?" asked Emil. "I gather he's held the land a long time?"

"Inherited it from his father," said Tom, "who inherited it from his own father. My dad was in the real estate business early in the century, and kept trying to get the Ryans to sell; but they were never interested. Charlie was born here in town, but he's lived in Europe for a long time and has kept up the family tradition, so to speak—he's held onto his land. He got rid of one small piece of property about thirty years ago, but nothing since, until just recently."

"How will the city accommodate all this growth?" asked Emil. "You must be planning to expand all your services—fire and police, sewer lines and trash disposal, library and schools and a hundred other things I'm forgetting."

"The Mayor set up a Task Force." said Bill, "which has made plans and started various projects, and some of the developers have agreed to buy the bonds that will finance a new sewer plant and city hall and a fire station and so on."

"Not everyone agrees with Bill that the city's growth'll be a disaster," said Cynthia. "A lot of us look forward to getting some new blood in the town; and of course the changes are likely to make our businessmen more prosperous, and will create new jobs."

"Some folks who have to commute into the city now," added Tom, "will find work here in La Aldea as clerks in new stores, or managers in new offices."

"They'll be able to walk to work, perhaps," said Bill, "but from the seeds of so-called progress they'll reap a harvest of traffic jams, and inexperienced teachers for their kids, and a lot of dust and dirt from construction, and murders and rapes where they had nothing worse than burglaries. They'll look back with nostalgia on the good old days when everyone knew and helped everyone else, and they'll wish nothing had changed. I should have written editorials opposing all this new construction, when the first building permits were being contemplated."

"I hope Abigail and Emil are observing the paradox," said Tom. "Our hot liberal, here, who usually favors change—who wants to ease moral standards so our schoolteacher can practice free love, and to force a labor union on our local entrepreneur—has become coldly conservative when it comes to La Aldean growth, and wants everything to stay as it always was."

Laughing Bill said, "And Mr. Valley, our icy reactionary, who usually favors the status quo—virginity and laissez-faire—is a flaming radical when it comes to La Aldean growth, and wants everything to change as rapidly as possible."

It's not so easy to laugh at yourself about things close to the bone, but they both were and it was nice to see and I thought I'd put in a pitch while Bill was so cheerful. "Between the flames and the ice we'll get frozen the same time we get suntanned," said I, "though I'm surprised to see how phlegm and choler spell off so neatly in you two. What I worry is how the fiery fury and the arctic anger can hurt the innocents who don't deserve it. Ms. Able is suffering, now the School Board complains and her life is the talk of La Aldea; and Mrs. Hooper and Elizabeth are tormented by the sad facts everyone learned today. Remembering those helpless, why not try to put all this behind us out of sight, and not keep dragging it out into the desert and the snow?"

"It's easier said than done," said Cynthia, "people being what they are. But you're right, of course. I'll be glad to promise never to bring up either scandal, and to change the subject if others do. Who'll join me?"

Caroline and Tom looked ready to jump but Bill saw the fence and shied. "Hold on now, one moment, Abigail," said he. "Hooper and Ms. Able are public figures, one an educator of our children, the other the employer of many of our citizens, so to the extent that their actions reflect on their character, those actions merit discussion in the community—and in its newspaper."

"But what does a responsible newspaper do in situations like these?" said Emil. "How is the public good affected by the romantic attachments of our citizens?"

It depended on the circumstances, and the School Board was unwisely attacking Ms. Able whose life was an open book and whose love didn't affect her job, while Hooper was cheating his wife and probably others as well was what Bill explained. No one not even Caroline liked this argument much but the Press isn't always thoughtful consistent when there's a good story around, so there was some more choler displayed before we finally cooled off and went on to other things until it was late.

Driving home Emil wondered, "Nice party. Tom Valley's a vigorous chap, for being so old. He must be in his seventies. And I'll bet he's making a pile of money, handling all that Ryan property."

"The good huckster knows his customers but I wonder how," said I.

"How he got Ryan's business? I don't know. I suppose he mostly keeps track of buyers and sellers here in town by being a part of Sadie's rumor mill. Down at The Cafe every morning he jokes with the boys, and drinks coffee, and hears who just got a promotion and might move away, or who's having another baby so they'll have to be looking for a bigger house. But with Ryan in Europe . . . of course, Tom said his own father knew Ryan's parents. Maybe that was the connection. Or maybe Tom and Ryan were friends before Ryan left town."

"Maybe. But I bet Valley's competition wonders how come just like I do." I changed the subject. "Remember that time in Paris?" I asked him because mentions of Europe always reminded me of kisses in a small gallery at the Louvre, and he hugged me so I knew he remembered.

Later in bed we exchanged stories of the day. He was pleased with his progress and I was with him, and there was some usual smooching before we drowsed off. As we went to sleep spooned I was thinking something was wrong somehow, but didn't know what it was and where.

CHAPTER 5

Tuesday Morning

I have never understood why opposites should attract. My courting of Abigail, years ago, was accompanied by a bustling and stirring, a sparkle and magic, an anxiety and regret, a heavy breathing and moist dreams which certainly did not stem from some awareness of how different we were. But if it had, where would the attraction have come from? Were we supposed to have perceived that our counteracting qualities would complement one another, making the couple greater than the sum of its parts? Or were the two of us each to have been intrigued and enchanted by ideas and manners so different from our own?

Balderdash, is what I say. We might as easily have been repelled as captivated by all the dissimilarities. For it's clear we are antipodes in many ways. Right from the first, for example, we saw that my habits are regular and hers haphazard. There is no system in her life. No plan. She wanders from place to situation to person to crisis to God knows what as if she were a dust particle blown by the winds of fate, not an intelligent being with a will, a brain, and a conscience. Our romance was founded on some mixture of admiration, astonishment, and fleshly magnetism, not on our incompatibilities.

So Tuesday morning I got up at six-thirty, as I always do, and had a shower and shaved and dressed, not knowing whether she would have breakfast with me or sleep 'till lunchtime. When I left she was still sprawled across the bed in lovely disarray. We're not as young as we were, but the curves of her calves, bosom, shoulders, and brow have the same effect on me they always did. I restrained myself, however, and left a note asking her to call me at the paper when she was up and around. I thought she might want the car, so I walked down to the Cafe.

Sadie greeted me cordially, and fed me a hearty and delicious breakfast. I half-expected to see Tom Valley and his buddies, but they hadn't arrived by the time I had finished, and I paid my bill and hurried up to the *Aldean* offices. It was quarter to eight when I let myself in with a key Virgil had loaned me, and I went upstairs and got to work. The PC to mini problem was fixed; how about transfers between PC's? Lots of possible bad transfers between PC's: from the Spare to Bowman's PC, to Virg, to Caroline, and Sally; from Virg to Bowman, Caroline, and Sally; from Bowman to Caroline and Sally, and between Caroline and Sally. I'd decided to begin by getting everything going on the spare computer. Once that PC was working properly, Virgil could use it while I was checking his—and so on until the job was finished.

I turned on the spare and had started creating a test document when Sally Jensen came in, looking a little worried just as she had the day before. "Good morning, Mr. Lime." she said.

"Emil," I said. "I'm Emil, not Mr. Lime. How's the farm story coming?" Abigail had told me about it, and about Sally's barmaid job.

"I still have a good bit to do," she said. "I've been out Interviewing this morning, and wanted to put some paragraphs together while it's all fresh in my mind. Farmers certainly get up early!"

She went to work, and I got up and turned on Virgil's PC, then returned to the spare and typed in a request to send my test document to him. I went back to Virgil's machine, and set it up to monitor transfers. Sure enough, there was my test document, being written on the screen. No problem there, apparently. However, just to be sure, I went back to the spare and wrote a short program to send twenty copies of the test message over to PC 01, just as fast as they could be sent. Returned to 01 to watch. Trouble. Machine 01 only got sixteen of the twenty. Back to the spare. No indication that anything went wrong—apparently it sent out all twenty. What happened to the other four?

Time to rub my chin and scratch my head. What are the possibilities? Something wrong with my short test program? Could be a programming fault of some kind. Or a circuit problem. What else could it be? Maybe my spare was sending its message all right, but it was going to the wrong place? That's easy to check; there's only one other place it could go, because only one other PC was turned on. I got up and went to look over Sally's shoulder.

"Can I try something?" I asked. "It'll only take a second."

"Help yourself," she said, and rolled her chair aside so I could get at the keyboard. I hit the Escape key, and asked to look at files transmitted from other computers. Sure enough, there were the four missing copies of my test document! I invoked the measures that would tell me the address of Sally's computer, and it was 01. She was supposed to be 04. There was the trouble: two computers with the same address. "Thanks," I said to Sally. "Those four test documents you've got are there by accident. You can erase them whenever you want. And let me know when you're leaving. I'll have to get inside and change the switches to give you the right address." She nodded and went back to work. I don't think she'd understood what I was talking about, but it didn't matter.

Next I went to Bowman's office, turned on his computer, number 00, and tried sending my test from the spare to him. Everything worked fine, but I quickly discovered that Bowman's machine couldn't transmit data to the spare. I figured the problem was probably in the message-originating part of the communication circuit board. I removed the board from Bowman's PC called the office of the dealer who supplied the cards, and told them I'd bring the card in for testing that afternoon.

By this time Sally was no longer using her PC, so I took the cover off and reset her address from 01 to 04. I ran more and finally confirmed that everything was working fine.

I went downstairs and looked into the mini room. The machine was on, and a tall, lean gentleman was bending over the printer, looking at the results of some calculation. Abigail had described Martin Neare to me, and I assumed it was he and introduced myself.

"Ah, yes," he said, "Mr. Lime. I made your wife's acquaintance yesterday." Everyone always remembers meeting Abigail, however brief the encounter. "I understand you are to cure our computer distempers. Amazing machines. I confess they continually astound me. The programs we've bought have made the accountant's job into child's play." He looked a little like a child himself, his eyes wide, his expression ingenuous. He was wearing an expensive-looking three-piece suit, blue with a thin white stripe. The severe, formal clothes contrasted absurdly with the casual dress of Bowman's other employees, and I wondered why he felt the need for such a disguise.

"I'm hoping to get your troubles cleared up," I said. "I want to test data transfers from the mini this morning. Will that be all right? It shouldn't interfere with what you're doing."

"I foresee no problem."

"And later on today, I want to look again at the page layout problem you're having. To do that, I'll have to have the mini to myself. What would be a good time for that, Mr. Neare?"

He rubbed his nose thoughtfully. "I believe any time after lunch would be convenient," he said. "I myself certainly will be finished here by then. But perhaps you should check also with Mr. Smith."

I told him I would, and went back upstairs. Bowman, Virgil, Caroline, and George had arrived while I was downstairs, and I said hello and went back to work on the spare PC. Ran half an hour's tests calling for data from the mini, and found nothing wrong.

Caroline was hard at work, but I interrupted her. "I've got the spare going now," I said. "Would you mind using it for a while, so I can check out your PC? Virg says it can't send or receive anything."

She gave me a bright smile and said she didn't mind. It took her a minute to dump her story onto a diskette, and to move over to the other machine. She was certainly a lovely woman, and was wearing a very pretty, very form-fitting cotton dress. I wrenched my attention back to business, and started testing her machine. After half an hour I found a fault in one of the cables—whoever had made the cable was careless or incompetent—the central wire had been cut so short it wasn't making contact. I unplugged the cable and put it with the card from Bowman's machine, ready to take to the dealer that afternoon.

Next, I asked Virg if he would mind using Caroline's PC while I checked out the word processing problem he had mentioned the day before. He didn't mind, and I took over. I soon found that Caroline's program wasn't compatible with Virg's. I installed the right program and found all was well—the nonsense characters had disappeared, and I had no trouble editing the story. Called Virg over, explained what had been wrong, and gave him a demonstration.

"It looks as if you forgot to run the installation program in the beginning," I said. "Either that, or you or someone installed it wrong."

He was disgusted. "Good lord," he said. "Should have figured that out myself. Thanks, Emil. How's everything else going?"

"I think I have a handle on everything except the layout program and the intermittent problem you mentioned you and Sally have. I'll need both your machines for a while to check that one out, and thought I'd come in early tomorrow morning to work on it. Neare said I could work with the mini on the layout problem right after lunch. That be all right with you?"

"How long will you be? The paper's out Thursday, you know. And we've got some layouts ready we want to do this afternoon."

"Could you give me an hour and a half? From one to two-thirty? I have to be in Woodland Hills at three—I've got some things to check out with your dealer." He agreed that would be satisfactory, and I went back to the spare PC—Caroline was using hers again.

I got the Instruction manual for the layout program, looked up the telephone number of PJA, the program designer, and gave them a call. "I'm working with the *Weekly Aldean*, a newspaper out here in California," I said, "and we've got a problem with your program. Can you connect me with someone in your technical support department?"

"One moment, please." All operators sound the same, and have the same script. After a pleasantly short time, a female voice said, "May I help you?"

I told her who I was and where, and described the problem briefly. "We lose stories," I said. "We ask the program to lay out from two to six stories on a page, and usually it works fine. But every few weeks—maybe once in fifty or a hundred layouts—it'll leave one story out, completely. And it'll show us a big blank space in the page. Have you ever seen this problem with any of your other customers?"

She said they hadn't, and that they had found the only way to resolve such troubles was to work with a diskette containing a sample of the difficulty—copies of the stories to be laid out. Could we send such a sample, along with a letter describing our installation: computer type, memory size, peripheral attachments, and so on? She wasn't willing to talk about the program itself and what might be wrong, and so I told her I'd try for a sample, and hung up.

I had some time before lunch, and thought I'd look through old diskettes for some more examples of faulty layouts. Maybe in trying them out on the mini in the afternoon I'd see something that would help me, or help PJA, track down the trouble. So I got a big boxful of diskettes from the archive file downstairs, and started going through them, searching for issues marked with an asterisk, and setting them aside when I found them. On the third such diskette, I discovered that one of the stories to be laid out was missing. That was strange—I'd noticed the same thing while I was looking the previous afternoon. This time I dug out of my tool kit a special program that tries to retrieve lost files. When I ran it, it recovered the missing story.

Now that was even stranger. I had assumed that the missing story had disappeared before the archive diskette was made up. But since the recovery program worked, obviously the lost story had once been there, on the archive disk, and had been erased at some point by someone who was looking at old stories. It was hard to see how that could happen. For one thing, each of the old diskettes was protected with a tab which prevented its being written on or erased. Someone would have to peel off the tab to delete a story, and then put the tab back on.

I dug out the diskette I had noted the previous night, and was able to recover the missing story there, too. That got me curious, and I began looking through all the archive disks, not only for layout problems, but for missing stories. I found a good many. It appeared somehow that one, and sometimes two stories were erased from about fifteen percent of the diskettes. I recovered all those I noticed. There were so many of them that I figured there must be some regular practice or routine someone was following which accidentally did the erasing.

By noon I had a dozen more examples of layout problems ready to try on the mini, and was ready for lunch. I started to call Abigail at the motel, but just then she showed up, and we went to the Cafe with Virgil and Caroline. Bowman was lunching at his desk again. While we ate I told them of the morning's progress, and asked Abigail if I could have the car to drive in to see the dealer that afternoon. She didn't mind. We ordered hamburgers (Virg and I) and salads (the girls), and discussed the missing stories, but no one had any ideas how they could have been erased.

"Everyone's been told to leave the write-protect tabs on the diskettes," Virg said, leaning back in his chair. "And we tell them why it's important. But sometimes we let outsiders look through past issues. Maybe we don't instruct them carefully enough."

"How often are the archive diskettes used?" I asked.

"Fairly often," Virg replied.

"Several times a month, I'd guess," Caroline added.

"Do you let anyone take them home, to use on their own PC'S?"

"That's not supposed to happen," Virg said. "But I suppose it could. You say you've recovered all the erased stories?"

"Probably not all of them, but a good many. Why?"

"I was wondering about that story I've been looking for. The one that talked about gold rings and raindrops. Might it be among those you've turned up?"

"It's possible," I said. I fished a paper out of my shirt pocket and handed it to him. "Here's a list of the disks I've checked. The ones where I recovered stories are circled. You could search them for rings, and see."

Abigail asked what this was about a jewelry story, and Virg told her of the skeleton and the raindrop ring and then added, "Maybe I'll have a look this afternoon, while you're out. Emil. But getting back to how the stories got erased in the first place . . . Are you sure the tab always works? Maybe you can delete something from a diskette, even when it's got its tab in place."

"It could be," I said. "There might be a PC where the circuit that's supposed to feel for the tab is out of order. But at the same time there would have to be an operator error or program bug that called for an erasure. It's very strange."

"Strange computers doing strange things is the story of your career, and the reason we've been able to send our children to college," Abigail said, "so you should be neither surprised nor sorry but expectant and welcoming. And we've had enough machines for now so let's talk about people or parachutes or polecats." And we did.

CHAPTER 6

Tuesday Afternoon

After lunch back to the office Emil gave me a peck on the cheek before back to work, but I claimed a better warmer one and left him happy hot and bothered. Upstairs George with Sally and three new ladies, so he introduced Mary, Roberta, and Alice, all part-timers like Sally. Mary was rawboned severe with glassy eyes; Roberta sparkling overflowed a Dior I thought it was; freckled Alice wore a ribbon in her hair and a jelly spot on her slacks. They seemed probably like me happy out with society, but will also be happy to be home quiet evenings.

"A regular harem I have here, Abigail," said George with a leer. "Veritable slaves they are, giving their all for the glory of journalism and a pittance of a salary."

Mary frowned. Roberta dimpled, and Alice flushed at all this heavy and unnecessary irony, but you have to remember his pictures and look behind what he says. "Do you each write columns like Caroline?" asked I.

George didn't give them time and said, "Roberta does high society, and tells us who's who and who isn't and why not; Mary has religion and churches, covering the one day in the week all our proper ladies put on their kid gloves; and Alice deals with food, including a recipe every week that's either delicious and unhealthful, or organic and inedible. Sally's assignment keeps changing—this week it's farming, but she handles architecture and gardening and God-knows-what-else. Every Tuesday afternoon they gather me up to tell me what pictures they'll need next week, and to complain about the ones I've got ready for Thursday's edition."

Standing around a table they moved aside and I could see how George had done it this time. Sally's farmer was dusty but pleased with himself and the field red with tomatoes and his house and barn behind. Mary's preacher wore a fine benign look and a flowered buttonhole behind the pulpit sermon just finished. Alice's lamb chops carrots mashed potatoes was composed on a heavy ornate plate on a fancy linen cloth on an old oak table. Roberta's visiting grandmother glasses on her nose bore a large smile with arms outstretched to hug the kids, while grandpa waited wistful just behind.

"Splendid stories made George take such pictures," said I, "and Bill Bowman is lucky hired such a crew. Do you all have second jobs, serving beers like Sally?"

Roberta got in before George this time, being gregarious answered for the three. "I don't." said she, "but Alice and Mary do—they run a typing and secretarial service over on Daffodil Street. I don't know how they manage their families and two jobs. My husband complains he gets short shrift, and I'm only here at the paper one day a week. But of course I spend a lot of time on the phone and in the town, chatting with folks."

Talked a while, and there were five churches with a lot of older people friendly and still very religious and good homemakers, liked to cook and party and garden and to read and talk about flowers and food, so the columns very popular. You could see it was old-fashioned, this town, ignored the year's swanky fads, no use for politics Washington or Sacramento. George they told me wrote every week on art, but he called it Pictures and signed it Vincent Van Rembrandt the whole town knew who *that* was. Then the ladies back to work and George to buy me a cup of coffee from the pot in the corner.

"What will be in pictures this week and should I call you Vincent?" said I when we were drinking the dreadful black stuff.

"The whole thing's a hangover from when I was young and foolish," said he. "This week I'm roasting a silly idiot who thinks different is the same as good. He's found a cockamamie gallery on La Cienega that feels the same way, and has mounted a show of star-shaped canvases each containing a colored circle with a kid's marble glued in the middle. I ask you, now. You don't have to look far to find something featherbrained calling itself art to write about these days." I wondered what had banged his life that he always found the world so sour sad, or was it twisted in his genes. To me the bad was the mad dog foaming you don't see every day, and I'd laugh at the kid's marbles not jeer, but then I'm not an artist and George is.

"How did you get gloomy cynical not bright hopeful?" asked I.

"None of your dam' business," he said.

"Business of all who admire you and great photos. Please."

"My hardware father and my artist mother," he said. "But it's my grubby ill nature, not their fault. Enough."

Likely himself didn't know, so back to Vincent's reviews.

"Is there nothing good you find for your column in LA or even anywhere?" said I.

"Not much. Anyway, saying good things ain't my style, as you must know by now, Abigail. What do you think of my little harem?"

"All a little worried but that could be the deadline feeling you've got when you're just married and the in-laws are coming to dinner the first time and you've never cooked a big dinner, or in high school when the book review is due tomorrow and you haven't started reading."

"Roberta's a gal never worries," said George. "She's Aldean High Society herself, and her old man is loaded. But the others are like I told you Sally is—scratching to make ends meet and wondering how they'll pay next month's bills on the gadgets and trivialities they dam' well shouldn't have bought anyway. They ought never to leave their houses without locking up their credit cards and checkbooks. Better still, they ought to be paid more."

He had something else, but during the Aldean High Society a door opened and Martin Neare shambled in to sit with us and a cup of coffee.

"Good afternoon, Mrs. Lime," said he settling down ignoring George. "Are you enjoying your visit to our little community?"

"From what I hear," said I, "it will not much longer be little, what with all the new houses being built the city's getting ready for."

"The dam' place'll never be the same again," said George.

"Ah, yes. *Tempus fugit*, as they say. But we are at the moment still an anachronism, out of step with the modern world." He seemed a small tall man, too proud of too little, but then George had said he was rich from the stock market even though he needed Caroline to help his arithmetic.

"Mr. Rawlins here and Mr. Bowman both old-time residents of La Aldea." said I using the Misters because of Mister Neare, "and you helped found the paper but are you a native too?"

"No, I am not," said he. "I spent my childhood In Arizona, and became acquainted with Mr. Bowman at college. He thought of me when he was inaugurating the paper, and required an accountant. For me, it was a fortunate happenstance. I have thrived, and I hope the paper has benefited from my services." He talked like a white-tie dinner party, and probably bowed before asking Mrs. Neare to accompany him to bed.

Talked a little more then excused myself wondered how to get to the city library. They told me where to walk to end my bookplace curiousity. Emil still below working so I waved, followed their easy directions only a few blocks. An old frame building probably once someone's house there was a librarian who looked she had been there thirty years. The history of the town, she said probably I should look at old copies of the *Weekly Aldean* for the Fifties on, and showed me them, but handle them carefully not on microfilm yet. I read back through New Paper for Community, and Wettest Thanksgiving Ever, and 1957 In Review, and Mayor Denies Alleged Bribe, and Volunteer Firemen Save Office, and Freeway Plans Will Affect City, and Garden Party at Ingram Home, and First Computer for La Aldea, and Beaten Wife Shoots Husband, and City Youth is Eagle Scout, and a score of others about the town when it was younger innocent, and so were we all, and a few more recent issues too.

Nearby a shelf of old City Directories back earlier to 1928. Showed all Aldea merchants the Bowmans and the Ryans and the Rawlins and the Valleys and the Hoopers and Helen Abernathy, but no Jitneys the motel owner must be new, and of course no Neares in the oldest books. Three Smiths but a very common name of course. Rawlins Hardware and Valley Real Estate but no businesses named Ryan or Bowman or Hooper.

Ms. Abernathy's new directory address not far away, and moseyed over to knock on her door another dignified old frame house and a big front porch.

"Yes?" from an old lady bent far over a cane old neat dress but with very bright eyes that had seen a lot of good and bad and would recognize trouble.

"My name is Abigail Lime just visiting town, and Caroline Bowman mentioned you've lived here a long time and remember everything," said I as if it was an introduction.

She pushed open the screen door and waved me in to polished pine floors with rag rugs and an upright piano and fringed lamps and matching legs on the chairs and the sofa and a ticking pendulum clock and lace doilies and fancy thimbles and dolls and children's games like jacks, and everywhere mementos like small ballet figures and an Empire State Building souvenir ashtray and photographs and framed testimonials and World Fair paperweights.

"Please sit down," said she and sat herself on the sofa. "I don't often have visitors from the outside world. What is it you would like me to remember, and why?"

She was old Mrs. Louckes my severe seventh-grade schoolteacher, so I sat very straight hands in my lap and behaved. "I'm just curious about La Aldea in the beginnings," said I, "but I can't explain exactly why something doesn't match up."

"What is the occasion of your visit here?" said she.

"I'm an idle woman with children grown and gone and follow my husband who has a job this week curing Bill Bowman's computers."

"And how have you come to conclude something isn't matching?"

"I've listened a lot when people talked and read some things and saw some others, but I can't yet finger a name for it except something seems not what it seems to be."

"You have an unconventional way of expressing yourself, Mrs. Lime. Improperly ungrammatical, yet effective. But you want to hear of early La Aldea?"

Sure enough Ms. Abernathy saw me just like old Mrs. Louckes, who appalled my English and graded my papers C—though she always knew what I meant. "Yes," said I. What was the start of it all?"

She looked the clock it was after 3:30 so "Would you please bring that decanter over here?" said she pointing. It was heavy cut glass and four snifters on a tray, and I put them on the small table next to her. "Will you join me in a glass of Scotch?". I yessed and she poured two and took a sip with a glad sigh. My sip was reluctant to keep company.

"I didn't come to town until 1924," said she, "so you must understand that much of what I'm telling you I have pieced together from occasional conversations over the years, and some study of old records. In the beginning, this whole valley on both sides of the main road from Woodland Hills towards Ventura was part of a Spanish land grant, and belonged to the Gutierrez family. It was a cattle ranch, mainly, though they raised crops enough to feed themselves and their dependents." Ninety she was Caroline said, but she was remembering like a schoolgirl in a history test. On she went.

"Then in the late eighteen-hundreds they began to sell off pieces of land. The ranch had been split between sons, and was no longer able to support everyone. The property that is now La Aldea and its surroundings was bought by a partnership of three men: Hiram Hill, James Belldick, and Clem Ryan. They were a strange assortment, and I don't know how they got together. Hill had come to California for gold, and struck it rich; Belldick was a ship-owner and trader; and Ryan, whose father was a wealthy Boston lawyer, was the black sheep son who unexpectedly inherited the family fortune when his parents and brothers were killed in a train accident.

"The partners subdivided part of their acquisition, and began trying to sell lots. Ryan married about that time, built a big house on the hill in back of town, and moved in; Hill and Belldick still lived in Los Angeles. The subdivision was not a success: La Aldea was too far from the city, there was no particular attraction like hot springs or a lake, and the landscape was not particularly captivating. The disappointed partners got to quarreling, and ultimately Ryan bought them out, at a price so low that Hill and Belldick felt they had been cheated.

"Time passed, and slowly other people bought lots, built homes, and moved in with their families. The population was only thirty in 1900; but by 1910 it was about 200, and in another twenty years it reached 2000. Since then, growth has been slow. In 1922 we incorporated, and in the next few years built a school and a small city hall. We were mostly a farming community, raising vegetables for the city markets. Water was always a problem, but there were some wells that supplied what we needed until finally we got access to Colorado River water.

"We've produced some illustrious citizens, and some deplorable ones. Mark Graham Campbell, the sculptor, was born here—his parents still live over on Peony Street. So were State Senator Sam Ilkins, and electronics genius Eddie Hooper. On the other hand, so was Natalie Peartree, the noted Madam who's now serving time for income tax evasion.

"Genius children often have a hard time even with wise parents," said I.

"Young Hooper, you mean. Eddie *did* have a hard time. He certainly wasn't popular in school," said she, "though he was too recalcitrant to be bullied. Instead, he was ostracized. Children don't like bookworms, it seems. His father was a plumber, and not a very successful one. Mr. Hooper and his wife loved classical music—that was the only indication I ever saw that the family was perhaps a little out of the ordinary."

"The founding father produced nobody prominent since you don't mention any Ryans," said I.

"That's right, as far as I know. The Ryans had six children, but were always stand-offish; they felt they were the town's elite, above hob-nobbing with people who lived down the hill. The eldest boy, Chester, was the only Ryan child who settled here. I don't really know what became of his brothers and sisters. He had married a girl he met when he was back East at college, and he inherited the big house when his parents died. He and his wife were not just snobbish, as his parents were. They were real recluses—were hardly ever seen to leave the house. Their only child, Charles, was actually born there, though the doctor had wanted Mrs. Ryan to go to the hospital in town. And then, strangely, they were killed in an accident, just as Clem Ryan's parents had been."

"Not another train wreck if they hardly ever left the house," said I.

"No. A fire. The old house on the hill burned down one night, and their bodies were found inside. Apparently there was a problem with the wiring, and by the time anyone noticed the flames and smoke, the house was almost gone."

"But their son Charlie wasn't hurt?" said I.

"He wasn't living at home—had an apartment somewhere here in town, as I remember. But it seemed the tragedy left its mark on him: not long after, as soon as the estate was settled, he left La Aldea and hasn't returned since. His home is in Europe now, the south of France, I believe."

"Bill Bowman a native son too so his parents moved here when the town was small?" said I.

"Yes. Greg Bowman was a mailman, then a supervisor of some kind in the Post Office, and Bill and his sister Grace both grew up here and graduated from the high school. Bill worked his way through college at Berkeley, and got a degree in journalism. Was with a paper out in the West Valley, I believe, before he started the *Weekly Aldean*. His sister married a lumberjack, and lives in Tacoma."

"The old city directories mention a Valley Real Estate company and a Rawlins Hardware but I couldn't be sure whether those are the fathers of Tom and George," said I.

Curious Ms. Abernathy looked at me to say, "You *have* been digging into our history, haven't you, Mrs. Lime. Valley Real Estate was started by Paul Valley, Tom's father, and Tom worked in the family business from the day he left school. Terence Rawlins founded and ran the town's hardware store, but young George took after his mother, and wasn't interested in nuts and bolts. She was very artistic—a painter, though not really a very good one. George discovered photography when he was a small boy, took pictures for the school paper, worked as a free-lance photographer for a while, and finally settled into his present job. His mother and I had wanted him to go to college, but his father didn't care, and George was a rebel and scoffed at us. He had two brothers, but I've lost track of them. His parents died years ago. They had sold the store, but it failed a few years back—competition from the big chains."

That agreed with George's telling but still no explanation his grumpy. All interesting but who knows whether helpful, and my head swimming a little from the whiskey I'm not used to. She had put the stopper back in the bottle with just the one drink. Evidently scotch a hobby not a profession, and I'd bothered her enough so after a while we said goodbye. "Come back," said she and I said I would and walked to the town center hoping not to stumble into a tree.

At the Cafe, Elizabeth Hooper with David for company. Glad to see me and to the park to bench sit and talk. "I tried to reach you at the motel, Mrs. Lime, but couldn't," and I said where while she twisted the ring on her finger. "I don't know what to do. Mother is still in bed and looks at the wall without saying anything. She told me she never wants to see Father again, and doesn't want me to see him. I know what he's done is terrible, but that isn't reasonable, is it? Can I never see my father?"

I told her it wasn't and she could, and we might go home and talk to Mother, maybe she'd change her mind. It was a new house with old antiques, and she was in bed upstairs.

"Mother, this is Mrs. Lime," said she. "You remember, I've told you about her. The lady whose husband is fixing Mr. Bowman's computers?"

Mother staring at the wall. Fancy clothes and thirty pairs of shoes at least showing there where the closet door wasn't closed, and not a book in sight. The bed a four-poster, and a spinning wheel of all things in the corner, and pewter pots and fancy old candlesticks and a landscape looked ancient and Dutch, though not on the wall she was staring at.

"My name Is Abigail," said I from a Captain's chair by the bed Elizabeth in another nearby, "the same as President John Adams' wife a long time ago. Some of your antiques look like they might be from her time."

She stirred maybe thinking about the past but didn't say a thing so I went over to the spinning wheel.

"My grandmother taught me how to spin, but I was a child and forget, now. She and grandfather had sheep once, but that was before I was born. My mother cooked but she never taught me." Still nothing, but she listened.

"I was called Abigail because my father was an innkeeper and a poet, liked old-fashioned names. Things were better in the past he thought." That was miles leagues centuries from the truth but he'd forgive me for fibbing in a good cause.

Mrs. Hooper stirred again, and said, "Life wasn't so hard, those days. Homes were more comfortable. There wasn't so much going to and fro. Children were better-behaved. Housework was easier."

"Housework?" said I thinking washboards and wood stoves and carrying water from the well.

"You just told the servants," said she, "and they cleaned and washed and marketed and cooked. And neighbors were more helpful. And husbands weren't away so much, travelling goodness knows where and being so mysterious about it."

Once she was talking, an hour of conversation sliding from old times to old friends to parties to card-playing to clothes, together with some sympathy that was easy because now was such a bad time for her, she was ready to get up and was beginning to think a husband's rascality might be the end of a marriage but not the world. I left them more cheerful, and at the front door Elizabeth thanked me grateful. She asked if I'd visit her father at the hospital tell him she hoped he felt better but Mother wouldn't let her come, and I said I would.

CHAPTER 7

Tuesday Afternoon

The hour and a half I spent that afternoon on the mini, puzzling over the layout problem, was both illuminating and gratifying. It's always pleasant to notice the glimmer other passers-by have missed, and thus to turn up the lost pearl. By that time I had over thirty diskettes containing examples of faulty composition, and I began by trying each one out on the Layout program. The symptoms were unchanged—the program was still losing one story from each page. But as I ran them, one after another, I realized they all had two things in common. First, each page was supposed to contain five or more stories; if a *Weekly Aldean* page had four or fewer articles, the Layout program always seemed able to handle it. And second, in each bad page the final, incomplete layout always split the first story between two columns, with the second column beginning in a short line, the end of a paragraph.

I knew enough about typesetting to know that printers hate to start a new column with such a short line. Their dislike is reflected in their use of the word "widow" to describe such a column, and I was sure the Layout program was written so that widows couldn't occur. So it seemed certain that there was some kind of a programming error which had to do with avoiding these 'widows'.

Having figured out what was probably wrong, I wondered whether I might find some way of outwitting the program until the PJA people got around to fixing their mistake. Looking at their Instruction Manual, I noticed that the operator had to set the page length in the beginning when the system was set up. The Weekly Aldean page was 102 lines long. I tried resetting the length to 101 lines and reran the thirty bad pages. Twenty-six of them worked perfectly, four reported "not enough room on the page", and one gave me a layout, but again with a story missing.

About that time Virg came in, and I explained what I had found. "I'll compose a letter to PJA describing the problem, and you can send it along with a diskette containing samples," I said. "That ought to give them enough evidence to go on, so they can fix it. Meanwhile, if you reset page length to 101 lines every time you have a missing story, I think you'll find the layout will work about three-quarters of the time."

"How do I change the page length?" he asked, and I showed him, reminding him he had to change it back to 102 for normal operations. By that time it was nearing two-thirty, and I went upstairs to pick up the bad card and cable, and headed off for my appointment with the computer dealer in Woodland Hills.

Woodland Hills is a pleasant, quiet town just south of Ventura Boulevard about twenty miles from La Aldea. The computer store was right on the boulevard. It had a big picture window not appropriate for computers, but just right for furniture or whatever had been sold there before. The dealer himself looked and sounded a little like a cowboy, in his blue jeans, boots, and 'Howdy', but he knew his business and was polite and helpful. He gave me a new cable, plugged the card into one of his own computers, and replaced it when it displayed the same symptoms it had shown me out in La Aldea. By a little after three-thirty I was back in the Aldean office. I passed a glowering George Rawlins on the stairs as I came in, but he ignored my greeting—as irascible as ever. Replaced the cable and card I had brought from town, and checked Caroline's and Bill's PC'S to be sure the replacements had cured their problems. They had.

When I had finished testing Bowman's system, I told him I thought I had everything solved except the intermittent trouble Virg had told me about, and that I'd work on it early the next morning.

"You've been very efficient," he said. "It's only Tuesday. I had thought it might take you a week or so to resolve all the difficulties."

"Well, I've been lucky so far. There haven't been any really nasty or tricky problems. And I haven't really cured your layout problem—I've just pinned it down so the PJA people can fix it. The problem I'll tackle tomorrow may turn out to be a monster that can only be killed with a week's analysis and a silver stake to drive through its heart."

Bowman laughed. "That's a remedy I'd like to administer to many of society's uncouth villains," he said. "But I hope our computers won't need such treatment."

"You just can't tell about those intermittent troubles. If they occur every minute, on the average, it's not so bad. In ten minutes you can collect ten examples, which should give you some idea of what's wrong. You install a fix, and run, and if ten minutes go by without anything bad happening, you figure you've probably cured your troubles. If you remove the fix and they come back, and then reinstall it and they disappear again, you're happy.

"But if the intermittent pops up once an hour, on the average, instead of once a minute. Then where are you?"

He thought about it. "I see," he said. "It'll take ten hours to collect ten samples, and at least an hour after you've put in a remedy before you discover whether your cure has been effective."

"Four or five hours, more likely. At the moment, I don't know how frequently Virg's problem crops up. I'll tell you tomorrow, after I've done some tests. But if it's anything like the 'missing file' problem, I'll have my hands full."

"'Missing file' problem? You mean the missing stories in layout?"

"No," I told him. "It's something else I turned up. Looking through your archive diskettes, I discovered some stories were missing. After a little investigation, I was able to recover them all, which means they had been on the diskettes originally, but had somehow been erased in the past few years."

"Erased? How could that happen? And why do you say they were 'erased', if you've found them again."

"The only way to be really sure something is erased on a disk is to re-format the disk—to make it like new. If you just erase a file, all the computer does is eliminate it from the directory—the file's still on the disk but you can't see or read it. So if you restore the directory entry, you can read the file again. But I don't know how such a thing could happen. It could be something intermittent, like a bad circuit in a disk drive somewhere." I got up. "Likely it'd be another monster to track down, and I don't propose to look into it unless you want me to. I'll show Virg how he can recover a missing story, and since it doesn't happen often, and just concerns your archives, I suggest you just live with it."

Bowman agreed that was the thing to do, waved me good-bye, and went back to work. I shut his door behind me, and looked around the bull pen, where I noticed Virg was frowning at his PC. I went over to ask whether he was having some kind of trouble—something I hadn't fixed?

"No trouble," he said, "I'm just searching those diskettes where you recovered files. I'm looking for that missing story." He pointed to a clipping on his desk. "There's the article that started me off." I picked it up and read:

SKELETON UNEARTHED AT GROUDBREAKING CEREMONY
Governor's Shovel Would Have Turned up Skull

Winslow, AZ, Apr. 17, 1986. Gov. Bruce Babbitt came to Winslow to take part in the beginnings of a big new hospital for this bright and arid city, and found himself looking at the remains of a man apparently dead for decades. The Governor was due to arrive at 9 a.m. to break ground at the site of the $23 million Marion Z. Silting Memorial Hospital, and workmen were cleaning up the area in preparation for his arrival.

"We had chopped down the weeds where the Governor was gonna dig," said Thomas Williams, foreman, "and were raking 'em into a pile, when I noticed a bone stickin' out of the ground." By the time Gov. Babbitt arrived, a skull had been uncovered along with several other bones, the police had taken charge, and the groundbreaking site had been moved a hundred feet west.

After viewing the remains, the Governor said, "We were too late to help him, whoever he was, but starting next year the Silting Hospital will be ready to help others from Winslow and neighboring communities."

Later in the day Chief of Police Arthur Prenditt reported that the skeleton was that of a young man, probably between twenty and thirty when he died. "It's likely he died in the early Fifties," he said. "We can't rule out foul play, though at first glance there is no damage of the kind you'd expect from a shooting or beating. The body was in an old stream bed, and the location, of course, is not far from Route 66, which was the main east-west highway thirty years ago."

The youth's clothing and personal identification had rotted away long ago. However, in excavating the area where the body was found, authorities unearthed several small coins dated 1950 and earlier, the rusted remnants of a few keys, and an unusual ring. The ring, made of solid gold, had a unique design consisting of a single, tear-shaped image in bas-relief on the surface—a raindrop, perhaps. "The ring is the only clue we have to the identity of the young man," said Chief Prenditt. "All we can do is hope that someone recognizes it and lets us know who it belonged to."

I looked over Virg's shoulder. His computer was finding rings and drops and rain and gold in various stories, but still nothing that was going to help the police in Arizona.

The spare PC was not in use, so I sat down at its keyboard and typed up my letter to PJA. Described all the symptoms I had seen, and explained what I thought the problem might be. I put Virg's name at the bottom, dug up some *Weekly Aldean* stationary, and printed out a copy for him to sign. When I brought it to him I saw he was obviously excited.

"I found it!" he said. "It must have been one of the 'lost' articles you recovered for us. But it tells a very surprising story. Have a look."

He motioned me to a chair, and moved aside so I could scroll the story down the screen as I read it. It was from the March 24, 1983, issue of the *Weekly Aldean*, was written by a Somers Grant, and was about Puns. "Grant was retired," Virg said. "He had been an English teacher here in town starting in the thirties. Occasionally he wrote articles for us. He died about two years ago. Go ahead and read the story; he mentions the ring in about the third paragraph."

I scrolled through, reading about puns. Mr. Grant was obviously an erudite man, and one with a puckish sense of humor. He began by describing puns as word-actors on the stage of wit, pretending to be something not themselves. He cited puns from Shakespeare and Joyce, and compared them with some he'd run across in his classrooms. He told how they have been deprecated and even hated by some, tolerated and even loved by others. In paragraph three he was discussing their use in art and decoration, and it was here Virg found the reference he had half-remembered: "Another example of the use of a pun as a witty design element could once be found right here in La Aldea. Clem Ryan, the Founder of our city, inherited a gold ring embossed with the image of a teardrop. Apparently there was a long history of Ryan ancestors whose first initial was C, and the tear, of course, was a pun on C. Ryan, or 'cryin'. I suppose Clem's son Chester, and then his grandson Charles inherited the ring when the old man died."

"So the ring in Arizona may be Clem Ryan's?" I asked.

Virg was back at the keyboard, requesting a printout of the story. "It could be," he said. "In fact, the skeleton could be Charlie Ryan's. He must have been in his twenties back in 1950."

"But I thought Ryan was still alive. Isn't he the one who's been selling off all his local property the past few years?"

"That's right. But it's said he lives in Europe. I don't know when it was anyone saw him last. The property sales have been handled through his bankers, in New York. Let's show this to Bill, and see what he says."

Virg tore off the printout of the story, went to Caroline's desk and spoke to her briefly, and the three of us went into Bowman's office. Bill was hard at work at his PC, busy with some story or editorial for Thursday's paper, but he invited us to sit down and asked what was up.

"You remember that wire-service story last year," Virg said, "about the skeleton they found in Arizona, and the raindrop ring? At the time, I told you it reminded me of something." He handed Bowman the listing. "I finally found the reference in an archive diskette, thanks to Emil. It was in old Mr. Grant's article on puns. Have a look at the third paragraph. In fact, read it out loud, because Caroline hasn't heard it yet." Bowman read it, frowning at first, then amazed.

"So one possibility," Virg said, "is that the Arizona skeleton is Charlie Ryan's."

"But how can that be?" Bowman asked. "Charlie just disposed of some land last year." He paused and thought for a minute. "But of course, nobody's actually seen him for a long time. He lives in France somewhere, I think. Tom Valley deals with him, but always through bankers in New York. Wonder when Tom saw him last . . . I suppose . . . He might be dead. But then who's impersonating him? Maybe he was killed, you think, and someone assumed his identity?"

"It's a possibility," said Virg. "He might have been murdered, even. It could be a whale of a story."

Bowman reached for his phone. "A story that'll put La Aldea on the map!" he said, and dialed. "Let's get Fred in on this. Hello, may I speak to the Chief? Fred? This is Bill Bowman. I've got a story here that you'll find interesting. It's complicated, but has to do with a mystery, a body, and maybe a murder. Can you come over to my office and hear about it? Good. See you in a few minutes." He hung up. "He'll be right over," he said, and then added for my benefit, "That was Fred O'Leary, our Chief of Police."

Just then there was a knock on the door, and Abigail came in. We found her a chair, and spent the next few minutes explaining what Virgil had discovered. Her reaction was not one of surprise, I could see. She was at the same time satisfied and worried. I couldn't figure her out, but then I never have been able to. She and I each see things the other doesn't. It's as if we look at every scene through two different windows. I see the facts and events, and infer their causes and effects; she sees the uncertainties, the shadows and hazards, and senses the circumstances around them.

Chief O'Leary arrived and was introduced to Abigail and me. He was a thick-set, ruddy-faced man in uniform, and his quick how-do-you-do, questioning eyes, and easy manners gave me the impression he was quite competent to look into this crazy story. I sat back to watch and listen.

CHAPTER 8

Tuesday Afternoon

Chief Fred arrived and Bill told him Emil was a fixer and I was along, and he got to work writing carefully in a dog-eared notebook. Looked at you when you talked and listened like he wanted to hear, so he had a chance of scraping the truths out of the bottom of this barrel.

"You may remember this article from the *Times* last year," said Bill starting things off, "about the skeleton they excavated in Arizona." He handed the clipping. "It mentions a very unusual ring found with the corpse, and Virg here has unearthed an article we published four years ago that describes a similar ring that once belonged to Clem Ryan, and presumably was inherited by his grandson Charlie. Of course, it's possibly just a coincidence, but it occurred to us that the Arizona ring might be the one in our article, and that the body might be Charlie's. That can be checked out, can't it, from dental records or something?"

"It could be, if we can find the records and if we think Ryan's dead," said Chief Fred remembering the story. "You have any reason for believing he's not alive? If I'm not mistaken, he's been selling property 'round town the past few years, and that's not easy for a dead man to do." He was still skeptical like me that time Emil calculated the house was cooler cold in summer with the windows closed, but skeptical is right in serious things like science and death.

"We realize that," said Bill. "But tell me: how long has it been since anyone's actually seen Charlie Ryan? He lives in Europe, I understand; he's been there for years—but who has actually laid eyes on him?" A little uncertain, since of course skeletons of people we think alive are as common as owls in scarlet or elephants playing marbles.

"I know it sounds unlikely," said Virg, "but the ring was unusual. A very distinctive design. Probably it was made to order a hundred years ago or more. It could be a duplicate or coincidence. Or it could have been stolen from Charlie Ryan or from his father or grandfather. But on the other hand, that might be Charlie's skeleton. Don't you think it's worth checking?"

You could tell the Chief would check but wanted to hear someone else explain why. "On the phone a few minutes ago you mentioned murder," said he to Bill. "Is there something you haven't told me that makes you think Ryan was murdered?"

"I think I was the one who first used that word," said Virg. "But it was just a guess or a hunch or something. We don't have any evidence."

"When was the last time anyone actually saw Ryan?" said Chief Fred and looked around at all of us like the family watchdog curious at new furniture in the living room, but nobody replied.

"As far as I know, he hasn't visited La Aldea in decades," said Bill after a minute, "but I can tell you when I last saw him. It was the day he left town, back in . . . "pause and thought" . . . in 1952 I guess it was. His parents had died not long before, and he had some money and said he was going to take a slow journey around the world. It was a wonderful opportunity for a young man. But since then, the one individual I know who has been in communication with him is Tom Valley, who's been selling Charlie's property. Even so, I don't think Tom's ever actually seen him since he left town."

"How about we get Tom over here so he can tell us?" said Chief Fred.

We watched while Bill phoned. Tom would be over in a few minutes.

"Who else might know about him?" said the Chief, which I was wondering too, so as to learn had Mr. Ryan been straitlaced or easygoing, careless or cautious, trustful or suspicious.

"Well of course he was before Caroline's and Virg's time," said Bill, "and before yours, for that matter. But a lot of old-timers must remember him; he was born and grew up here, and went to school with all of us. George Rawlins would remember him, and my ex-wife Jill, and Elmer Wilkins, and the Hoopers, and Roberta Orr, and dozens of people, though I don't know whether anyone has been in correspondence with him. In fact, if he had dealings with anyone, I should think it would be me. We were pretty good friends—were actually sharing an apartment when his mother and father died in the fire, and when he left town."

"You've never had a letter or phone call or card or anything from him?" said Chief Fred.

"No," said Bill. "When he went away he said he'd write, but he . . . wait a minute. I think I did get one post card from him, from Barstow or somewhere soon after he left, but that was all. It didn't worry me, not hearing from him, because I was busy and I figured he was enjoying what he was doing, and was putting his past life behind him. He had never really liked La Aldea—his contemporaries had never treated him well, and the death of his parents was a terrible blow." It's hard being an orphan unexpectedly when everybody you loved died but you were still depending on them and hadn't got around to thanks. I was lucky my father and mother went easily but not together, and knew their grandchildren and that they'd shaped us right.

"You still have the card?"

"Lord, no. I only vaguely remember it. Must have tossed it as soon as I'd read it."

"Do you remember Ryan's wearing this teardrop ring?"

"I've been thinking about that," said Bill, "and I'm pretty sure he wasn't wearing it, those days. I remember his wearing the high school ring a few years earlier—we all did—but by the time he took off, I don't believe either of us was wearing a ring of any kind. Certainly he'd never told me the story of the pun on his name; and I didn't read Grant's article about it, for otherwise I would have remembered when I saw this Arizona story last year."

"You didn't read the story in your own newspaper?" said Chief Fred.

"I hardly ever read all the stories," said Bill laughing because the world thinks editors read everything and chefs eat everything and tailors wear everything. "By the time this week's edition is out, I'm working on next week's, and sometimes I'm away travelling, and there is always a bunch of books and magazines I'm trying to find time for."

"Somers Grant's article was mine," said Caroline. "I mean, he brought it in and I talked to him and read it and accepted it and did a little editing. Bill and I discussed it at the time, but there was no reason for him to read it." She blushed to apologize, "I'm the one should have remembered about the ring in his story."

Just then Tom Valley was there and the room was crowded with another chair, and Chief Fred explained the skeleton and the pun. "Do you remember Ryan having the ring?" asked he.

Tom shook his head frowning and said, "I hardly knew Charlie Ryan. Or his folks either. They were a quiet bunch, kept to themselves. And I'm another generation, almost, ten years older than Charlie. I was out in the hard world selling real estate with my father when he and Bill, here, were still in high school. But what are you saying? It can't be Charlie Ryan's body. I've been selling Charlie's property for him these past five years or so."

"When was the last time you saw him?"

"Saw him? Well . . . I don't remember. Must have been before he left town and settled in Europe, years ago. But I've had letters from him from time to time. And of course he has to sign real estate contracts and deeds and so on."

"You still have all the letters?"

"Oh, yes. There's a big Ryan file at the office, and whatever he's written is there. So what are you saying? That someone's impersonating him? Good Lord. If he's dead, what's the legal position of all the people who've been buying his land?"

"How are the sales handled?" said Chief Fred. "How does the money change hands, and where are the papers signed?"

"It's all done from New York, through the DuPair Manhattan Bank. Charlie lives in France, I believe, but he seems to do a lot of travelling, and when he's in New York he meets with a banker named Dubroski. I understand Ryan keeps deeds and other important papers in a safe deposit box there at the bank, where he transacts all his legal business, and where the money is deposited." I was thinking it's where the *love* of that money is deposited that will cause the trouble, and then smiled thinking how Emil frowns my extravagances but always pays the bills.

"Does Dubroski know where Ryan lives? How does he get in touch with him when he needs to?"

Tom didn't know that, but he knew the bank's address and telephone and the banker's full name which all got in Chief Fred's notebook before the next question.

"Is there still more property to be sold?"

"Two more pieces," said Tom. "He's been selling tracts and lots one at a time, and we sold the most recent one about six months ago. I expect I'll hear soon about which one to sell next."

"When did he start selling?"

Tom figured a moment before the answer. "It was in '82, as I remember. Of course, he sold the first piece long ago, way back in the Fifties."

Chief Fred was surprised but Tom had told us at dinner so we knew. "In the Fifties! Which year was that?"

"I don't remember, exactly," said Tom. "I can look it up. He would have done better to have held on to it—he didn't get much in those days. But I suppose he needed the money."

"I remember he had quite a wallet full when he left," said Bill, "mostly in travelers' checks. He figured it was enough to take him around the world, hitchhiking and camping out and spending as little as possible." Hitching in those days easier than today, with so many folks on both side of the thumb forgetting about Doing unto Others.

"What did he do with the deeds to all that property when he took off? Do you know?"

"Yes," said Bill, "I was just going to say that he had them last time I saw him, and told me he planned to leave them in the bank on his way out of town."

"If he had deposited them here in the bank," said Chief Fred, "he must have come back for them and someone would have seen him. I can check on that. Most likely he forgot in the excitement of leaving, or he got a lucky ride out of town and didn't have time to stop. So either he dropped them off at some other bank on the way for safekeeping, or he would have had the deeds with him when he hit Arizona."

"He'd need more money at some point," said Caroline, "and might have sold off that piece of property for cash. Unless he found a job of some kind."

"Or unless he was dead," said Chief Fred. "How did he come to choose Valley Real Estate to do business with, Tom? Do you know?"

"I have no Idea. He may have remembered my father talking to his, when they were boys. I think the file will show we had a letter from someone at the bank—it wasn't Dubroski back then—forwarding a letter from Ryan which authorized us—specifically mentioned Valley Real Estate by name—to list and sell that first piece of property. The banker said he was holding the deed, and any news about offers for the property should be sent to him."

"But if Ryan was dead, the impersonator must have chosen you to handle the sale. I wonder where he got your name."

"Maybe the banker did some checking, and recommended us," said Tom.

"Maybe the impersonator looked in the phone book. He could have picked out a firm at random," said Virg.

"How many realtors were there in town those days?" said Emil always looking for numbers.

Shrugging, "I don't remember exactly," said Tom. "Certainly five of us, at least."

"Valley must be near the end of the listing in the yellow pages," said Emil likely right about that but his next remark wasn't, because people aren't so straightforward. "You'd think someone choosing from there would pick the first name."

"That piece of property he sold in the Fifties," said Chief Fred, "was it the best one to sell first? Could someone who hadn't been In La Aldea have chosen it?"

"Well, I don't know If it was the 'best' one to sell," said Tom. "I don't know what that means. But what he did was sell the smallest one."

"Maybe he could tell from the deeds which was smallest," said Chief Fred talking to himself now and we all listened. "But why not sell a bigger one? Why not sell them all? Unless he knew enough about it to suspect the property would appreciate if he waited long enough. Do you remember, Tom, did anyone come through town looking at land the weeks before you heard from that banker the first time?"

"Good heavens, Fred," said Tom. "That was thirty years ago or more. How would I remember? Certainly people did pass through in those days looking for land to buy. La Aldea is located beautifully to participate in the growth of the San Fernando Valley. But there's no way of knowing whether your 'impersonator' was one of them."

"Yeah." said Chief Fred, "and I'm ahead of myself anyway. We don't know for sure Charlie Ryan is dead. That's the first thing to check. I'll call Dubroski at the bank in New York, explain the situation, and see whether he can put us in touch with Ryan, in Europe or wherever he is. And I'll talk to Chief Prenditt in Arizona and try to connect the body to Ryan. Do you or Bill know who his dentist was? The easiest thing would be to compare dental records."

"I don't recall his going to a dentist," said Bill, "but I've just remembered one thing that might help. Anyone who was around those days would tell you that Charlie once broke his arm in a most comical accident. It was just after school, and he was on his bicycle, and all the kids were there, talking and starting for home. As usual, the family dogs were around greeting their owners, and one shaggy, giant beast was a favorite with everyone. He was very friendly, and had the personality of an old vaudeville actor—I swear he'd do double-takes, and could grin at jokes and leer at the girls. Well, Charlie wasn't looking where he was going, ran his bike right into the dog, tumbled over the handlebars, and broke his arm. He was sitting there on the pavement, holding onto the arm in obvious pain, and the dog came up, sat right in front of him and shook its head, sadly, as if to comment on the stupidity of man. And we all remembered it because of the head-shaking, and because the damned dog's name happened to be Armbuster. Poor Charlie took a lot of ribbing after we helped him to his feet and took him to the doctor."

"Another pun on pitiful Charlie," said I wondering whether *all* the kids laughed and how Charlie felt probably a shy boy.

"Which arm was it," said Chief Fred.

"I'm fairly certain he was right-handed, and the accident put him out of action for weeks—so it was his right arm."

Chief Fred stood up stretched said, "I guess that gives me enough to go on for now. If he's still alive we'll find out and Arizona will still have a mystery. If we can prove it's his body, then maybe he was murdered by someone who knew he had the deeds on him and figured to profit by them, or maybe he was killed for small change by a thug who then found the deeds and disposed of them, or maybe he died of a heart attack and someone found the papers and sold or used them. We'll see."

"When will you know something?" said Bill. "We want to keep right on top of this."

"I dunno. I'll get on the phone right away, but you know how these things go."

"Virg," said Bill, "if it turns out that's Charlie's body, we want a story, page one in this week's paper, so will you take it? Keep in touch with Fred, and dig up anything you can about Charlie from old-timers. Also, let's ask our readers if any of them have seen him since he left town—maybe some one's run into him in Europe, or New York or somewhere. Depending on what turns up, we may be able to sell the story to the wire services."

Chief Fred turned just leaving at the door. "Let me know if you find out anything that'll help," said he and left.

"I've got to talk to Horace," said Tom Valley frowning like a plowed field. "I've got to ask him who will be suing who if it turns out I've been selling a dead man's property." So Horace must be his lawyer and Tom scurried out the White Rabbit.

"Who should I interview?" said Virg ignoring Tom and his worries. "You mentioned Roberta and Elmer and Jill would remember Charlie. Anybody else?"

"George would," said Bill, "and the Hoopers—we were all at school at the same time. Maybe some of the old-timers would remember him, or better yet would remember his parents or even his grandparents." He thought and saw how the story would grow. "Come to think of it, I remember now that Charlie's grandfather, I think it was, was one of the town founders, and that's how Charlie inherited all the property. You'll have to dig out that part of the story, too."

"You might talk to Mrs. Abernathy." said Caroline. "She's been around long enough, and she was Town Clerk so . . ."

"I talked to her this afternoon," said I interrupting, "all about Clem Ryan and James Belldick and Hiram Hill and buying the land from the Gutierrez family, so you can get her details."

They looked at me surprised how come I was asking about Aldean history before I knew about Charlie's death. "I was just curious after Bill explained the town stalled 'till Charlie started to sell his land. Are there any Hills or Belldicks in town nowadays, or relatives of theirs? Mrs. Abernathy said they owned property thought Clem Ryan cheated them."

No one knew, and we all sat a while longer while Bill and Virgil and Caroline talked the story and how to do it looking under all the rocks. Virg so engrossed he forgot Caroline was pretty to look at but Emil kept peeking so I took his hand and we said goodbye to go off to dinner and he could peek debauch at me instead, and I would tell him we had to visit Mr. Hooper at the hospital.

It's good young girls still smite him, showing his heart is not as old as the rest of us.

CHAPTER 9

Tuesday Evening

My wife can be very annoying. She had something on her mind about Charlie Ryan, but I couldn't get her to tell me what it was.

"You were rubbing your ankle in there," I said when we left Bowman's office that afternoon. "What's going on?" She knows that I know she sits with one shoe slipped off, scratching the other ankle with her big toe, when she's thinking about something that puzzles her.

"A young fellow should win out Adonis or not," she said. Virg wasn't exactly handsome, but he wasn't ugly either. And of course Bill Bowman was dignified, accomplished, distinguished—a man of parts.

"Sometimes beautiful girls like you and Caroline are attracted to us older men," I said, trying not to smirk, and wondering what Virg had to do with her puzzlement.

"Charlie might small, but a stranger never would," Abigail said. Might small what, and would what? Sometimes her riddles are more obscure than they are other times.

"How can you be so sure that's Ryan's body?" I asked. "Maybe the banker has given Fred his address and telephone number by now, and the Chief has talked to him."

"If they find the right one it'll be broken." She was referring to the skeleton's arm, of course.

"What in blazes makes you think so?" I said.

"La Aldea's gestalt is dead if Charlie's alive," she said. "Let's have dinner now and we've got a call to make this evening and there'll be more to find out tomorrow."

"Gestalt!" I said. "When did you become an expert on gestalt? And who're we going to call on?" But I couldn't get her to say anything more. She would be infuriatingly exasperating if her damned eyelashes weren't so long.

As we talked we passed through the big empty bull pen and headed down the stairs. At the front door we ran into Martin Neare, apparently on his way out.

"Good afternoon," he said, holding the door open for us. "Leaving for the day, I presume. Has your investigation of our computer problem progressed to your satisfaction?"

"Yes," I said. "I've fixed several things, and really have only one major ailment left to cure, so far as I know. But the past hour or two we've . . ."

"That's a car of great beauty you have, Mr. Neare," Abigail said, and walked over to admire the big, cream-colored Cadillac parked by the curb. She took my arm. "Emil, if you were as generous as you are handsome, would I have a car so fancy?"

"What kind of a question is that?" I said with my indignation on the rise. But of course Abigail hardly knows one car from another and doesn't like to drive anyway, so I saw she was playing some sort of game. "We can't afford such a fancy vehicle," I added a bit uncertainly, and got my arm squeezed in a way that told me I'd apparently said the right thing.

"May I be permitted to drop you off somewhere?" Neare asked. "I'd be delighted to have the opportunity to show you how comfortable the car is."

"Why, that would be lovely. Is there a place not far where we could have a cocktail? And . . . and would you have time to join drink with us?" She was looking a little lost and lonesome, waif-like, as if she hated the thought of having to spend an evening stuck alone with her dull husband, and Neare bit on it like he was an albacore and she an anchovy. He unlocked the car door and held it open for her.

"I shall make the time, Mrs. Lime. Mrs. Neare isn't expecting me for another half-hour." He hustled around to the driver's seat, leaving me to climb in next to Abigail with my quizzical look, which she ignored. "The Village Inn is not far," Neare said, "and I can take a circuitous route which will enable me to display for you the beauties of our city while you sample the luxuriousness of my automobile." I got the impression the old windbag might have parked in a dark dead-end street and made a pass at Abigail if I hadn't been along. His verbiage was directed at her, and he ignored me.

"I haven't really seen the nicer parts of town much," she said. "We had dinner with the Bowmans last night very pleasant, but mostly I've just wandered around old Main Street."

Neare turned on Gardenia and headed up into the foothills. "The best residential area overlooks the city from the west," he said. "This first portion I'll show you was originally developed in the early years of the century." He drove around, showing us where the Mayor lived, and Tom Valley, and the President of the local bank. We passed a very pleasant park, and circled the large and well-landscaped reservoir which supplies the town with water. On the way back down, he pointed out his own house.

"It looks a very comfortable place," Abigail said. "Have you always lived there?"

"No, we moved in 1983," Neare replied. "Up until that time, we had occupied a modest apartment on B Street." I remembered B Street. It was in the oldest part of town, and all the buildings in that area deserved the adjective 'modest'. I suddenly saw what Abigail was thinking about. The Neares had moved into an expensive house in 1983, and the imposter had started selling off more of Ryan's property in 1982. I wondered when Neare had bought his Cadillac.

"Mrs. Neare must have been pleased, coming onto the hill. We wives always love to move up in the world, delighted when the success of our husbands makes life more luxurious relaxing."

"I hope and believe Mrs. Neare was satisfied. It was a rewarding time for us."

"It must have been," Abigail said, "with a new house and a fine car, the lords of luck were with you."

"It wasn't precisely luck," Neare said.

"What, then, was the source foundation of your good fortune?"

"I had made a prudent investment in the Stock Market in 1981. The Chrysler Corporation was in straitened circumstances, and I bought all the stock I could with our modest savings. The speculation was amply repaid, and has made possible a notable change in our way of life."

"Chrysler changed your life," I remarked, "but your car is built by General Motors. Seems a little surprising."

"I invested in an automobile acknowledged to be the best in the world," Neare replied warmly, if a little inaccurately.

"And a very comfortable car it is," Abigail said before I could reply. We had turned onto Main Street again. "I'm thirsty now ready for that drink. Thank you very much for the tour of the town, Mr. Neare, which showed us things we'd have never seen nor heard of."

The Village Inn was dim but cheerful, and served dinner as well as drinks. We went to the bar, and I had a beer while Neare and Abigail drank Manhattans.

"I believe Mr. O'Leary visited our offices this afternoon," Neare remarked when we had been served.

"Yes," Abigail replied. "Emil's computer checkup has led to an unexpected diagnosis about an old Aldean which he should tell you."

Neare looked at me for an explanation, and I told him what we had uncovered that afternoon. He remembered the story about the skeleton, but said he had not read the article on puns.

"What a remarkable coincidence," he said, ". . . I mean, the ring being found, and Mr. Grant's remembering the pun on Mr. Ryan's name. But surely that's all it is—coincidence. I'm confident Mr. O'Leary will find that Mr. Ryan is alive and well."

"Why do you say that?" I asked.

"Well, the alternative seems to be that someone dishonest has been selling his property all these years. Such things happen on TV, but surely not here in our pleasant town."

"You're right, of course," Abigail put in. "But until the Chief talks to Charlie Ryan and punctures our balloon of mystery and intrigue, we are all stretching our imaginations like the old dog stretches his back in the early morning, and finds villains behind every bush. Bill Bowman shared an apartment with Charlie, knew him better than anyone; and Tom Valley can't explain why his firm was chosen to sell the property; and Edward Hooper unexpectedly got money financing his electronics business; and George Rawlins always has resented being poor; and you . . . let's see. I know. You were living in Arizona when the body was found there, weren't you, Mr. Neare?"

Neare looked more and more disturbed as Abigail's recital of possible villains went on, and by the time she got to the question, he was stiff with indignation and resentment. "Really, Mrs. Lime," he said, "I don't see how . . . imagination is all very well, but . . . Mr. Bowman and Mr. Valley and Mr. Hooper? Arizona? I *did* work in Arizona after college, but I certainly . . . How could I have known Mr. Ryan? I was not acquainted with La Aldea in those days, except of course I knew Mr. Bowman at school and knew this was his home. What . . ."

"Please, Mr. Neare," Abigail said, smiling her most disarming smile, which would liquefy the heart of a hungry shark. "You forget we are just stretching our imaginations, so you should say where you were working in Arizona and then explain why Emil and I are probably the swindlers."

"I was employed in various cities around the state, but I don't find your insinuations amusing in the least." He was obviously upset, and drank down the rest of his Manhattan in one gulp. "Now I really must get on home. Mrs. Neare will be wondering where I am. Good evening." And before either of us could say a thing, he was up and away and out the door.

When he was out of sight, Abigail turned to me with a giggle. "Do the guilty ones always look so guilty, or the innocent?" she asked me.

"I do *not* understand you, Abigail. What in the world makes you think the imposter lives here in La Aldea? Or are you just playing games? If that's it, you scared old Neare out of his eyeshades and suspenders."

"Just some more gestalt. But Mr. Neare deserves what he got, waylaying us at the office to find what the Chief wanted. So where shall we have dinner before we go to the hospital?"

"Hospital!" I said, and she explained she had promised Elizabeth we'd visit her father tonight, to find out how he was and to tell him why Elizabeth herself couldn't come.

We decided we'd eat there at the Inn, and after finishing our drinks left the bar and got the hostess to seat us in the dining room. The waitress was just taking our order when Virgil Smith came in the front door. I waved to him, and he came over and accepted our invitation to join us for dinner. We all ordered, and I asked,

"What've you been up to? Anything new?"

"I've been making phone calls," he replied. "There isn't much to report. Talked to Jill Bowman and Mrs. Hooper. Have an appointment to see Mrs. Abernathy tomorrow morning. I couldn't reach George—don't know where he is. But no one I've talked to has seen Ryan. No one's even heard from him since the early Fifties. The fire killed his parents in April of '51. I stopped by the library, and found the story in the *Fernando Valley News.*"

"So probably Ryan left here in Fifty-two?" I asked. "That's what Bill guessed—the year after the fire."

"Did the story mention any Ryan relatives besides son Charlie?" Abigail asked.

"No. And no Ryans except Charlie were at the funeral. Bill was there. Of course, the Ryans were his roommate's parents. But I didn't recognize any other names." He paused a moment, then added, "That's not quite true. There was another spectator we all know: George Rawlins was there. His name wasn't on the list of attendees, but the story included a picture of the funeral. George was the photographer."

"No Hills in the company, or Belldicks?" Abigail asked.

"Actually, the article about the fire was also an obit. It said something about Charlie's father's life. Chester, his name was. And then it talked about his grandfather Clem. Told how he and some friends bought land and got the city started. It mentioned Hill and Belldick, but I'm sure neither of them was at the funeral. Hardly anyone was there. Chester Ryan and his wife were apparently real hermits. Had very few friends. The obit said the Ryans were 'very private people, who kept to themselves.'"

"Caroline's a lovely girl," Abigail said, and I wondered what brought on that *non sequitur*. Virg was obviously puzzled, too.

"Yes, of course," he said, "but what has that got to do . . ."

"How did you let her get away from you, a young vigorous fella but she married practically a grandfather?"

Virg was half puzzled, half indignant, and half embarrassed, even though that is really too many halves for an engineer to count. "Come on, Abigail," he said. "How come these personal questions? What does all this have to do with Charlie Ryan?"

"Then though Caroline is lovely you're not young vigorous and didn't care?"

"Caroline is charming. She's also Mrs. Bowman and I was only a dumb reporter, damn it! She hardly noticed me. But you haven't said—what does Caroline have to do with Ryan?"

"Caroline noticed you I know and was disappointed you faded in the stretch, young Virgil. But you want a question has to do with Charlie: who exactly has inspected the old *Weekly Aldean* archive diskettes the past years?"

Virg looked at me and rolled his eyes, and I rolled my eyes right back at him. Abigail laughed at us, and said, "Terrible how you two have to put up with an erratic typical fluffy-headed woman but answer me anyway."

"Well, anyone who works for the paper can use the archives any time," Virg said. "Outsiders have to come ask for help. They're supposed to sign a sort of log. But what does that have to do with Charlie Ryan?"

"She's wondering whether someone here in town might have erased Somers Grant's article on puns," I said. "But a lot of stories were erased, and there are a lot of other possible explanations."

"Never-you-mind," Abigail said. "Can we go look at the log?"

Virg shrugged. "Sure, if you like. I have to go back to the office, anyway."

We finished our dinners, talking of this and that but mostly of Ryan and his apparent death. I paid the bill, and Virg drove us back to the office. The log he had mentioned was downstairs, near the cabinet where the archive diskettes were kept, and we had a look. It was in a loose-leaf notebook, and was obviously pretty informal. There were a lot of names we didn't recognize, but we also saw Chief O'Leary, Tom and Cynthia Valley, Fire Chief Elmer Wilkins, and Sam likens, the state senator. I wondered what they'd all been looking up.

"Everybody but Ed Hooper," Abigail remarked.

Virg was surprised, and turned the book so he could look. "Didn't he sign? I'm sure he used the archives at least once. I remember Martin was showing him where they were, and how to read them."

"Martin?" I said. "Martin Neare? I had the impression Neare's feeling for computers was like Mrs. Lincoln's feeling for the theater. Does he actually know how to turn a PC on and insert a diskette and request a search and so on?"

"Oh, yes. I know he gives the impression that he's absent-minded. But sometimes Martin surprises you. He took a course, or read a book or something. Managed to learn enough to do all the elementary things, at any rate."

Abigail wanted to make a phone call, so she went upstairs while Virg and I talked about Neare. He had heard Martin made some money on the market, but hadn't heard about the Chrysler stock. When Abigail came back we told Virg good-night and went out to the car.

"Whom did you call, and where are we off to?" I asked.

"Over to Buttercup, out to Eighth and we'll meet Jill Bowman."

I started the car and followed her instructions. "Is Ms. Bowman a suspect? A possible murderess and imposter and embezzler?"

"And accomplice and provider of stories of days gone by," was the reply. I should have known I wasn't going to get a sensible answer, since I hadn't asked a sensible question. I tried another tack.

"Do you suppose Neare really made his money investing in Chrysler?"

"He told it knowing it could be checked but whoever's guilty will be caught when Chief O'Leary knows where to dig."

"He seems such a weak sister. What would have made him invest all his savings in a company about to go under?"

"He's a Croesusphile," Abigail said, "and it didn't go under, it came up." And with that we drove up Eighth Street in silence, me wondering whether there was such a word.

The front porch light was on at a comfortable-looking house, and we walked up and rang the bell. Young David Bowman opened the door and greeted us, with a special shy smile for Abigail, who had been so kind to Elizabeth. He took us to the living room, a room typical of California tract houses, and introduced his mother. Jill Bowman was a slim, pleasant lady with gray in her hair and a sort of wearily cheerful look in her eyes. She got us seated on a sofa which faced Norman Rockwell reproductions on the wall, asked if we'd like something to drink, and when we declined, said,

"You wanted to know something about Charlie Ryan, Mrs. Lime?"

"Please call us Abigail and Emil, and yes we heard you were in his class in high school."

"David told me the rumors flying around about Charlie's maybe being dead, and there's someone impersonating him, selling all his property. Could that be true?"

"The Police Chief is looking into it," I said. "It's not certain at this point, but it surely seems possible," and I went on to explain roughly what had been discovered, and how.

"Well, why are you asking questions? Isn't it a police matter? And why do you think I might have anything worthwhile to tell you?" She was looking at me, and of course I was innocent of wanting to ask questions, or at least of asking to come to see her that evening. But Abigail came to my rescue.

"It's my curiosity bump," she said, "and I am like the chipmunk at a new peanut tree can't help myself. Poor Emil puts up with me only because it's been a long time, and we're going to see Ed Hooper next for the same thing and to tell him why Elizabeth can't come. Do you remember Charlie Ryan?"

Ms. Bowman was a little confused by Abigail's syntax, but she recovered, and gave in. "Oh, yes," she said. "There were only about thirty of us in the whole class, so everyone knew everyone else."

"What was he like?"

"Well, he was very shy, for one thing, that's what I remember most. He lived way up on the hill, there, and rode his bike to and from school every day, all by himself."

"He didn't have any particular friends?"

"No, he didn't. When we were younger, in grammar school, the meaner boys used to tease him a lot, called him 'sissy', and wouldn't let him join their games, and pushed him around. But by high school we'd all grown up more, and he was—well, tolerated, if not liked."

"He didn't have a girl friend?"

"I don't think he ever even had a date, though I might be wrong. I don't remember him at any of the school dances. I remember seeing him at the movies once in a while with his parents."

"What did he do, summers?"

"Summers? Well, let's see. It was over forty years ago, you know. Nineteen forty-five, we graduated. Some of us had to work, summers. David's father and I always had some kind of job. He'd usually work up at the lumber yard when there was nothing doing up at Santa Barbara around the boats; and I'd be in somebody's office, typing and filing. George Rawlins worked at the stationers, which was also the camera shop, and developed pictures. The kids whose folks were well-off spent a lot of time across the mountains, at the beach. But Charlie . . . I'm sure he didn't have a job. I don't remember just what he did in the summer."

"Was he good in school, with a favorite teacher?"

"He wasn't a straight-A student, like Ed Hooper. But now that you mention it, he had a favorite subject and teacher. Charlie liked History, and there was a Mrs. Pearlstein who taught it and used to encourage him and gave him special books to read. I remember he almost lost his shyness, in History class. He wasn't reluctant to speak up, and ask questions, or even express an unusual point of view. And he really doted on Mrs. Pearlstein."

"Is Mrs. Pearlstein still around?" I asked. "Maybe she could tell us something about him."

"She moved away years ago. Have no idea where she went."

"How did Charlie and Bill become friends?" I asked. "They were sharing an apartment when Ryan's parents were killed in the fire."

"I really don't know. Bill and I dated in high school, but then we drifted apart, and I didn't see much of him for the next twenty years. I married, but that was a mistake and didn't last long, and then I worked and lived in LA. I wasn't living here in town in the Fifties, which I guess was when Bill and Charlie roomed together."

"Do you have a picture of Charlie in those days?" Abigail asked.

"No. I have an old snapshot album, but I don't think . . . wait a minute. Somewhere I have a copy of the school annual." She got up and headed for the door. "Just a sec. Let's see whether I can find it."

"Do you think somebody here in La Aldea killed Mr. Ryan?" David asked Abigail when his mother had gone.

"I don't think so don't know, David, but it's a strange and wonderful story, the Skeleton and the Ring like something out of Tom Sawyer or maybe Dickens or the Hobbit."

"And it'll fade like the coast fog burning off on a hot day," I said, "when Charlie turns up saying, 'What's all the fuss?'"

David said, "But it all fits—the ring, and the 1950 coins, and . . ." and then Jill returned, and his musing was interrupted.

"Here we are," she said, putting the book down on the coffee table and opening it. We all leaned over to look. It was a thin book with a fancy cover on which was embossed, "Aldean Alligators, Class of '45". The pages were glossy and filled with photographs, both of individuals and of groups: the chess, badminton, debating, and French clubs, the football and baseball teams, the scholarship society, the class officers, the Thespians, and a dozen more. There were signatures and greetings inked in everywhere.

"Bill was class President and on the swim team," Jill said. As she spoke, she was turning the pages and pointing out faces in the pictures. "Laurie MacArlie—she's Laurie Albany, the mayor's wife, now—was class secretary and president of the Girls' League. She and Bill and George and Ed Hooper were all in the scholarship society, but then so was I. George was a debater and photographer for the school paper, and Ed was a chess player. I was on the girls' volleyball team. Charlie . . . I guess Charlie wasn't in any of the clubs. But here's his picture."

She had turned to the two pages where the Individual portraits appeared. There were twenty-nine in the class, and I could recognize Bill and George and Jill, even without looking at the names printed below. George looked as cross then as now, Bill was on the plump side, even in those days, and Jill was a real beauty. Charlie Ryan's picture was right next to George's. He was thin and dark-haired, and the photographer had caught him with his forehead slightly wrinkled, as if he had just thought of something to worry about. Ed Hooper, on the opposite page with Bill, had curly hair and an aggressive look, almost as if he were hoping you'd say something he could take exception to. But though the individual images each told some kind of story, the feeling you had, looking at them, was that they were from another place, and that none of us today could understand them.

Abigail turned the pages, reading aloud some of the inscriptions: "I'll bet you'll go far, baby—Ed Hooper"; "To La Aldea's loveliest. Bill"; "Don't take any wooden nickels. George Rawlins"; "Hope you'll have all the best in the world!! Laurie MacArlle". She pointed out that Charlie had signed his name near his picture—just his name, in a very small script, with no greeting or petition for a happy future.

"No comment," Jill said, "but that was like him. You know how it is with those year-books. The last week of school, or maybe the last day, you carry them around with you and exchange them so as to sign your name and say something. I don't remember, really, but I'll bet we all had to twist Charlie's arm to get him to sign. He wouldn't volunteer. He'd be afraid someone would say they didn't want his old signature."

"Do you remember the time he broke his arm fell off his bike with the dog?" Abigail asked.

Jill smiled, but a little sadly. "Oh, yes. Armbuster," she said. "That's a story we all remember. But that was why Charlie was the way he was. We were always laughing at him."

We talked a while longer, but Abigail got up before long and reminded me we had another stop to make. We thanked Jill for her help, and I asked how to get to the hospital, and we were on our way.

"Well," I said as we drove back down the hill, "did we learn anything?"

"Charlie wrote small like many folks not happy do, and I wonder what Ed Hooper will be like all truculent forbidding."

I didn't know, but figured we'd soon find out. He was an engineer, so undoubtedly he would be wise, civilized, and genteel. His recent troubles with an irate husband indicated he must also be more than a little horny.

CHAPTER 10

Tuesday Evening

I put my head on his comfortable shoulder driving down the hill and over to the hospital. Emil knows he attracts the ladies or some, but he thinks the wrong reasons. Not his face a little overlined, not his figure a little stringy gaunt, not his small talk too elegant logical, not his out-of-date charm. It's his sort of wistful desire for affection, and a sturdy kindness some girls can see behind the gruff and I saw the minute I saw him. He figures he's lucky with me and I with him too, but he has more to put up with than I.

We had to get back on the freeway to get there, and it was a while before the parking lot and a quick walk in the warm dark to Visitors' Entrance. The helpful grayhead desk lady told us Ed Hooper was room 422, and we caught the elevator and found it. Knocked and went in and he was in bed in hospital room anonymous like them all, hair still curly very red though nearly sixty, reading some engineering magazine scowling.

"Who the hell are you?" said he. Bandage on his left ear and ugly bruises on his cheeks and forehead and one eye still half shut, but evidently he was recovering.

"Elizabeth asked us to visit," said I before Emil could be indignant. "I'm Abigail Lime and my husband Emil is fixing Bill Bowman's computers."

"Busybody Bowman. Be careful. Get your fees paid in advance. I have no use for him. He's a critic who knows nothing of how things work." Looking at Emil, "I don't meet many palindromes," then back at me, "How is Elizabeth? And my wife?"

It's strange the technical ones notice Emil's name oftener than the literary ones. "They're worried distraught," said I. "Florence didn't want Elizabeth to visit, so she asked and I've come to bring her love."

"I'm not sure you deserve it," said Emil and that wasn't necessary.

"It's none of your damn business, is it?" said Bowman would like to give Emil some of his bruises.

"She's a lovely and loving girl," said I, "and doesn't understand the world yet, or her father's affair. Would you like us to take her a message?"

"Tell her I've written a letter," said he. "She'll get it in a couple of days. In fact . . ." he debated with himself ". . . here. You take it to her," and he fished a letter, all sealed and stamped, out of his bedside drawer gave it to me.

"We'll see she gets it tonight," said I. "Have you written to Florence?"

He looked uncomfortable, like a child asked about Christmas thank-you notes in April. "No. What's there to say? She's a silly woman."

"What do you call a man who marries a silly woman?" asked Emil a good question but not politic.

"An idiot," said Bowman not hesitating.

"People change," said I. "Was she silly your wedding day?"

"Nope," said he. "She was naive and I was optimistic. As I got more cynical she got less practical."

"The cynic sees thunder and lightning in the same cloud where the optimist finds the silver lining," said I.

"That's right," said he. "An accurate observation. And the lightning is real, and kills. The silver lining Is a damn symbol. Never paid off a mortgage or bought a loaf of bread."

"Hiding under the bed from every cloud you're safe from storms," said I, "but never see the rainbows or get washed by warm spring showers. Maybe Florence . . ."

"Okay, okay," said he. "Enough. You and Florence stick to your warm spring showers. I'll hide under the bed and put up lightning rods."

"Many optimists use umbrellas and raincoats and lightning rods and rubber boots and sou'westers, and maybe Florence would quit hiding if you would."

"Hiding? I'm not hiding. I'm a realist. Grab what I can when I can," said he then changed the subject. "I hear you two have something to do with the Charlie Ryan mystery." It wasn't surprising, all over town and he must talk often with his office.

"I recovered a bunch of mislaid stories," said Emil, "and Virg Smith located the one that told of the tear-drop ring. You knew Ryan in high school, I gather. Tell us about him."

"Tell you what? Where he is? Who killed him? Whether he's dead? He was a nobody. Afraid of his shadow. Not very bright. Ate jelly sandwiches at noon out of a lunch box, for Christ's sake! Threw a ball like a girl. Wore those black clips on his legs when he rode his bike. Could hardly add two numbers together. Get the picture?" Picture of Hooper's self-satisfied bigoted intolerance, the brilliant engineer impatient with the inept, and blind to how complicated people are, including his wife and long ago Charlie Ryan, who maybe wore black clips but hurt when bullies teased him and liked history, which itself is full of bullies.

"Did he have any particular friends?" asked Emil.

"None I remember. Who'd be friends with such a jerk?"

"He was sharing an apartment with Bill Bowman when his parents died in that fire," said Emil.

"That figures. Creeps of a feather flocking together. Hey! Maybe Bowman killed him! You thought of that? Be just like him, talking sweet and doing dirty."

"You seem very sure Ryan is dead," said Emil.

"Looks likely. And Bowman his roommate . . ."

"Charlie left town in 1952 so do you know was Bill Bowman in Arizona then?" said I.

"Probably he was. How would I know?"

"In fifty-two where were you?" said I.

"Me? I was working for Douglas. Down in Santa Monica."

"So you were nearby," said Emil, "and are as good a murder suspect as Bowman is."

"Come off it! I'd been away at school. Wasn't diddling around with high school buddies in '52."

"Your parents were still living in La Aldea then?" said I.

"Oh, yeah. Until the sixties, when they both died."

"So you visited them sometimes," said I, "and heard about classmates, and could have given Charlie a ride leaving town, and could have financed Hooper Electronics selling Charlie's land."

"Yeah, sure. Could have started World War Two by bombing Pearl Harbor, too. But I didn't. Never gave Ryan a ride. Never went to Arizona. Got the money from venture capitalists. Investors. You could check it out."

"But you put up some of the money yourself?" said Emil.

"Sure. Some of it. Used all my savings. But you'd better be careful, accusing me of murder and larceny. I'll sic my lawyers on you. Sue for every dime you've got."

Emil shrugged. "You accused Bowman." said he. "We'd both better be careful. Who are those investors that we can check out?"

"Go to hell. None of your business."

"Virgil said you've looked at the newspaper computer archives," said I, "but he didn't know what for. What for?"

"Smith's a liar. He's Bowman's toady. But I dunno. Maybe I did look at them sometime. Don't remember. What difference does it make?"

"Somebody erased the story that told about Charlie Ryan's ring," said Emil. "We thought you might have some idea as to how it could have happened."

"Or that I might have done it myself? Horsecrap. But you recovered it after it was erased. That proves it wasn't me. I would've copied the diskette after erasing. You can't recover from a copy. Only a jackass would think the erase command destroys the file. Jackass like Bowman."

"Or somebody smart but in a hurry, who didn't think anyone would know how to retrieve an erased document," said Emil. "If Bowman hadn't hired me, and if I hadn't accidently noticed the missing files, no one would ever have connected the skeleton with Charlie Ryan."

"You're a regular hero, aren't you?"

Emil turned red. He'll not be meek to inherit the earth when a Hooper comes along to provoke him, so before he found the handle to fly off I got up and said, "We'll have to go to give Elizabeth her letter before bedtime so good-bye, Mr. Hooper. Interesting to meet you." I grabbed Emil's hand so as to shut off angry remarks.

"Hardly anyone is pleased to meet me," said Hooper. "Good-bye. Tell Elizabeth . . . tell her I'm not sorry. But I hope she forgives me. Keep in mind that your friend Bowman is a prime murder suspect. And don't stand under any silver-lined clouds."

Emil glowered at him and we left, and in the hall the cool was blown.

"I have seldom met a more disagreeable, uncouth, obnoxious, offensive, detestable individual in all my born days," said he. "He hasn't a good opinion of anyone except himself."

"And Elizabeth," said I, then to tease him cheerful, "Seemed a typical engineer. Logical, candid, favors reason over emotion, just like you. Notice the insult that crowned all, 'He could hardly add two numbers together.'"

"Abigail! I'm not like that. I enjoy people. I like Bowman, for example, even if I agree with Hooper that he's a bit wooly-headed. An engineer can be logical and still keep an open mind."

"If you enjoy people why not Mr. Hooper? Keep a logical open mind there. Hard to do it'll be good practice."

"You'd want me to find the good parts of Attila the Hun and the Marquis de Sade," he grumbled.

"Enjoy not admire," said I.

"How can anyone take pleasure in a boor?" said he. "For that matter, how can one really enjoy a person without admiring him?"

"Shylock? Jimmy Carter and Richard Nixon? Moriarty? Talleyrand? Mussolini? Fagin? Polonius? Billy Martin and John McEnroe . . . ?"

Got him laughing and he interrupted. "Stop, stop. What a collection. All right. I give up, and will try to enjoy Hooper. What makes people of his stripe, anyway?"

"He thinks the world is false self-serving, we think it bighearted honest. The world is both, but what did we see growing our biases?"

"And what is it mostly like, where we ourselves live and work?" said Emil. "Trouble is, I work in the same business Hooper does, but I don't see a lot of dishonesty and hypocrisy in it."

"We're optimists, but nevertheless we know somebody, maybe Mr. Hooper, stole Charlie Ryan's property."

In the car back to the Hooper house we argued possibilities until we arrived. I rang the doorbell and Elizabeth answered and I gave her the letter, finger to my lips so she put it in her pocket. I asked could we talk to her mother. In the living room she was leafing a magazine, so we interrupted and introduced Emil. She smiled a little vacant told us to sit down.

"We won't stay long," said I. "I just wanted to see if there's anything I can do."

"I've been trying to decide on a wardrobe for the Fall," said she gesturing at the magazine so she wasn't facing things she had to face.

"What're the pros and cons?" said I.

"I don't like the bright colors. When we were first married, Ed liked me in beige and soft orange and different browns. We lived in Culver City, near the movie studios. He was home almost every night for dinner."

"He didn't travel so much in those days?" said I.

"We visited his family here in La Aldea. But he was hardly ever away. Just a convention or two every year, in Chicago, or Las Vegas, or New York. We waited a long time for Elizabeth. By the time she came he was travelling more." She smiled wistful at her daughter who got up to kneel near and give a hug.

Elizabeth was doing right, and they'd somehow get through so, we said goodnight and left. On the way back to the hotel I stayed very close to Emil so he'd know I thought I was lucky optimistic, and tucked in our room we soon drifted off to sleep not worrying anything.

CHAPTER 11

Wednesday Morning

Wednesday morning I wanted to get an early start, and Abigail was still asleep when I left the motel. I was waiting on Sadie's doorstep when she opened the Cafe at six thirty.

"Did you hear?" she said after she sat me down and was pouring my coffee. "George Rawlins has quit the paper! He and Bill Bowman had some sort of big fight, and George told him to go to hell. But the biggest news is about that skeleton in Arizona. It looks like it's definitely Charlie's. Its right arm was broken sometime. And they figured out how he was killed." There were sure no secrets in La Aldea.

"How did they do that?"

"They dug around some more, and found the stomach bones or something. The pelvis, that's what it was. And it was broken in a way that made 'em think he was hit by a car or truck—a big, fast thingumabob. What'll you have to eat?"

I asked for bacon and eggs, and she put in the order and came back.

"There was never an accident report, so it looks like it must o' been a hit and run, and the driver must o' made off with the deeds and stuff. Right now the Chief's lookin' for the dental records to be absolutely sure, and is callin' that banker in New York."

"Tell me more about George," I said. "Did he really quit, or was he fired?"

"Bill told Caroline he quit," she said, "but o' course, in the heat of things, who knows what really happened?"

"And what were they fighting about?" I asked. "Did you hear?"

"It was somethin' to do about runnin' the paper. Now, why do you suppose George got into that? None of his bizness."

She was full of news and speculation, mostly about Ryan's skeleton, and I listened and, when she'd brought my food, thought about it. It could still be murder, I figured. Charlie could have got a ride with someone, and told him about the deeds and what they were worth, and the driver then could have arranged an accident and made off with the valuables. Or it could have been a real accident, where the driver stopped to try to help, found Charlie was dead, panicked, carried the body off the road and stole everything on it. Then was the driver also the impersonator, or did he sell or give the deeds to someone who did the impersonating? Whichever way it was, whoever got the papers either had to learn something about La Aldea, or had to be someone who already knew—who knew the property was valuable and would appreciate, and who knew Valley Realty would be a good outfit to sell it.

It wasn't likely that some chance Arizona driver would also be a La Aldea expert. So either he became an expert later, or he sold the deeds to someone who was or who became an expert. Or maybe he was a La Aldean who planned the whole thing and murdered Charlie.

There were too many possibilities to try to sort them out in my head, and I had things to do at the paper. So I finished my breakfast and walked over to the Aldean offices.

Bowman and Caroline were already there, hard at work, and it wasn't long before Virg arrived and the three of them went into conference to discuss the Ryan story. I was to tackle the intermittent problem on Caroline's and Virg's PC'S that morning, so I ignored the mystery and sat down at the keyboard.

Virg had said there were occasional errors when he tried to send something to Caroline, or she to him. I hadn't seen any examples in the short time I worked with the system, but that's what you expect with "occasional" problems. So I composed a small program which would alternately send a test message to and receive one from another computer. I installed the program on the two PC'S, and then set them to work. As soon as there was an error, or a missing message, I'd see a warning printed on the screen at Virg's PC.

While I waited it occurred to me that Wednesday was a day the wire service was broadcast. Had the repair I installed Monday cured the problems the mini had been having, receiving those stories? I went over to the spare PC and requested that the mini send up the stories as it received them, and watched the screen for a while. It looked good—no "scrambled" stories. My resoldering had done a cure.

I also finished checking other PC to PC transfers, and found no more problems.

So I could sit back and mull over the Ryan story again.

One way to look at it was to distinguish two crimes: Charlie's death, and the theft of his property by impersonation. The two crimes could be committed by the same person, or by two different people, and the criminal or criminals could be either La Aldeans or strangers. I drew up a little table of the six possibilities:

One Person		Two People			
Local	Stranger	Local Local	Local Stranger	Stranger Local	Stranger Stranger
1	2	3	4	5	6

Looking at the combinations, I decided that numbers 3, 4, and 5 were pretty unlikely. If a local—a La Aldean—were responsible for Charlie's death, surely he'd be the one to do the impersonation. He wouldn't recruit another local, nor would he get rid of the papers to some stranger. So 3 and 4 were superseded by 1. And if a stranger were responsible, either he'd do the impersonating himself, or he'd get rid of the deeds to another stranger. How would he locate someone criminally inclined in La Aldea? So 5 was very unlikely, and we were left with 1, 2, and 6. Either someone from La Aldea killed Charlie (by accident or on purpose) and since then has impersonated him—that's 1; or he was killed by a stranger who either himself saw the possibilities, impersonated Charlie, and sold the properties—that's 2—or by a stranger who disposed of the deeds in some way (maybe to a fence?) so that some other stranger did the impersonating and was reaping the profits—that's 6.

Of course, I wasn't on really firm ground in eliminating the middle three. But I could always come back to them if the other possibilities led me nowhere.

The best way to tackle number one, the La Aldean criminal, would be to check alibis. Who could have been in Arizona at the time of Charlie's death? Fred would look into that, but it would seem to be pretty difficult, and probably impossible. The time of death wasn't known exactly, and it all happened over thirty years before. In any event, how could it have taken place? Did the local person meet Charlie by accident out in Arizona, and see his opportunity to murder him and thus steal the real estate? That required the coincidence of their meeting, which seemed improbable. It seemed more likely that he would have been leaving La Aldea on a trip at the same time Charlie was, so that he could have offered Charlie a ride, or arranged to hitch-hike with him. Charlie hadn't mentioned such a fellow-traveler to Bowman when he was leaving; but maybe he hadn't turned up until the last minute. Or maybe Bowman was the traveler!

It seemed more likely that one or more strangers were involved. But if the impersonator were not from La Aldea, how did he know the property was valuable? He must have come here and had a look. He could have visited various realtors, pretending to be a potential buyer. Then he could have figured La Aldea would grow and that his deeds would make him rich in time, and he could have picked Tom Valley to handle the sales. From that point, he need never return again. Of course, that told us something about the stranger: he had to be presentable, to look at property and deal with bankers—he couldn't very well be a bum; he had to have some business judgment and experience; and he had to be patient to wait decades for the property to appreciate. He sounded like a confidence man, not a killer. And that, then, pointed to possibility six on my table. Maybe some low-life, half drunk, had hit and killed Charlie, who'd been walking along the road. Maybe he'd stopped, in a panic, moved the body to one side, and had taken Charlie's things, including the deeds. Maybe he'd given them to a friend, or got rid of them to his local fence. The deeds could have passed from hand to hand until they reached a con artist of some kind, who visited La Aldea to size up the situation, then sold one lot for some ready cash and put the rest away against his retirement.

While all this heavy thought was exercising my brain, my test program had been running and had found no trouble in either PC. Virg was back at work, over at the spare computer, and I interrupted him to ask, first, about George.

"I don't know any more than Sadie told you," he said. "No one's seen or talked to George since yesterday. I gather he hasn't been back to his apartment. And no one knows where he is."

That wasn't much news, so I turned to business and told him I couldn't duplicate his problem and asked if he could describe it to me more precisely.

"I don't know. Emil," he said. "I'll send something to Caroline. And then I'll get things from her. And once in a while something will arrive all garbled. All jumbled up on the screen."

I thanked him, and went back to his computer grumbling at my chowder head. The program I had been running would find missing messages, and would let me know if errors had been detected. But as I've mentioned, the test I wrote detected errors before they got to the PC screen—the circuits intercepted them, and the bad messages were retransmitted until they were received correctly. Virg was saying he actually was seeing scrambled messages on the screen, so most likely there was something wrong between the error-detecting circuits and the display. My program wouldn't find problems like that. It's as if I were a general getting messages from another general a continent away over a very sophisticated radio system that never made a mistake, and the messages were transcribed for me locally by a lazy private on an old Underwood typewriter. My original program just checked to see that the radio system was working, not what the private typed. I changed it so it also compared the message sent with the one displayed—in other words, so that it also checked whether the private with his Underwood might be making mistakes. Loaded the new program in both machines, and started them running again.

I watched while messages passed back and forth without error for a few minutes, and then got thinking about the stories that'd been erased from the archive diskettes. One way that could have happened was for some PC to have a faulty tab detector. So in the next few minutes, I managed to borrow each computer in the office long enough to try erasing a diskette equipped with a "write-protect" tab. All the attempts failed, so the erasures must have happened some other way.

About the time I'd finished that test, Fred 0'Leary arrived to see Bill Bowman. Caroline and Virg joined them, and no one complained when I stepped in to listen. The message-passing computers didn't need me. They'd keep records of any mistakes they detected.

"I wanted to give you a report on what I've found," the Chief said, "and ask some more questions. I've kept Virg informed about most of this, but bear with me while I go through it again. It'll help clear my thoughts." I noticed Virgil was taking notes. "First of all, it seems very likely that the skeleton in Arizona is Ryan's. It had had a broken right arm at one time, and its general description fits. Furthermore, we've found the dental records—they were in a box in Mrs. Rouse's attic, the dentist's widow. We'll be sending them off, but I'll bet they check out.

"The next piece of news is, that Ryan was probably hit by a car or truck. After that newspaper article was published, they found some more of the skeleton with broken bones. However, there never was a report of an accident, so we can assume it was a hit-and-run. They didn't find any suitcase remains at the site, so we can guess the driver stopped, moved the body off the road, and carried away whatever baggage Charlie had. Chief Prenditt has no leads or suspects, of course. And we're the first folks that ever called him with a believable story about the ring—apparently he had a lot of calls from people who hoped to claim it for the gold, but couldn't prove it was theirs.

"About the deeds, it seems Ryan didn't ever open a safe deposit box here in La Aldea. At least, no one remembers him opening one, and there's no record of one. He couldn't have left them in your apartment, could he, Bill?"

"I would have discovered them when I finally moved. But he hadn't left a thing. No clothes, books, papers—nothing. Maybe that helps explain why I wasn't surprised he never returned to La Aldea: he hadn't left anything to come back for."

"So he probably had them with him when he was killed. Now for New York. I talked to Dubroski this morning, and got a lot of questions answered. He sees Ryan, or the person who passes himself off as Ryan, whenever a deed has to be signed, but he has no address for the man. From time to time he gets letters, directing that he sell this or that piece of property, but the letters are from various places, mostly in Europe and sometimes the States. He said he'll try cabling the Swiss bank where the money is transferred, but he thinks it's unlikely they'll disclose an address. Our fake-Charlie is playing it very smart, and won't lead us to his home.

"The first piece of property was sold in 1956, and was handled by Dubroski's predecessor. The bank records show that it brought $47,000 net, that some $20,000 was withdrawn, and that the remainder stayed in the DuPair bank, drawing interest. The bank acted as trustee for fake Charlie, and filled out tax forms for him and paid his taxes—both income taxes to the Feds and the State, and property taxes to Ventura County here.

"Then in 1982 fake Charlie shows up again and authorizes the sale of another piece of property. In a few months it sold, and in '83 he has the bank transfer most of the proceeds to an account in a bank in Switzerland. In the past five years, our impersonator has transferred over three million dollars out of the country. He only left enough so Dubroski and the New York bank, still acting as trustee, could pay his taxes."

"If the bank was making out his tax forms all these years," I said, "did Ryan tell them of any income other than from the sale of La Aldea property? Or did he pretend his entire livelihood came from those proceeds?"

"I didn't ask," the Chief said, "but I'll bet no other income was ever included. Our impersonator wouldn't add anything that could point the finger at him." He thought about it. "It's a good point, though. I'll check next time I talk to Dubroski."

"If Charlie is dead, who are his heirs?" Virg asked. "Who is it that should have inherited the property? In other words, who does all that money really belong to?"

"We've just started looking into that," Fred said, "but I don't think we'll have any luck. Charlie's father, Chester, had five brothers and sisters, and apparently his grandfather's brothers died in a train accident. Chester and his wife kept very much to themselves, but even if they had been in touch with relatives, any addresses or records they had were destroyed in the fire almost forty years ago. Probably some

Ryan cousins are the true heirs, but we don't know how to reach them.

"But I told you I had some questions for you folks. Let me ask them, now. The article about the skeleton and the ring appeared in the paper almost a year ago. How come you didn't come to me then with the story about the puns? How come you only remembered Somers Grant's article yesterday?"

"That is a little embarrassing," Bowman said, "though we might ask why you—or for that matter, any Aldean subscriber—didn't recall the pun when the skeleton story was published. Our minds don't retain everything, or don't always match what's in our memories with what we learn." He went on to explain about Virg's vaguely remembering the story, and about the diskette searches.

"I heard something like that had happened," Fred said. Probably someone had told Sadie, and she had passed it on. "What I want to know is, how did that story get erased? Could it have been done on purpose by someone who didn't want the body identified—by the impersonator, for example?"

Everyone was quiet a minute, digesting this idea, though of course I'd already been thinking about it. Finally Bowman said, "Emil, you're the computer expert. Why don't you answer Fred?"

"Well," I said, "let me tell you about the diskette erasures as I see them. Every edition of the Weekly Aldean is stored on a disk just after the paper goes to press. The disks are kept downstairs, and are referred to occasionally by members of the staff and, I gather, by people from the town. This week I discovered that some stories, from some diskettes, had been erased—about thirty of them altogether, including the article on puns."

"Are you sure they had been put away on the disks in the first place?" the Chief asked.

"There can be no doubt about that," I replied. "That's how I was able to recover them. As I've told Bill, when the program 'erases' a story on a disk, it doesn't really destroy the story. All it does is remove it from the directory, so that normally it can't be found. So all you have to do is restore the directory, and your story is back."

"And the question is, who did the erasing?" the Chief asked.

"That's the question, all right. But it's one I can't answer. Each archive diskette has a tab on it which is supposed to prevent anyone from erasing it. So to eliminate those thirty stories, either the tabs had to be removed, or there had to be a PC somewhere with a faulty tab detector."

"Could one of the computers here be the culprit?"

"I've checked all the PC's here in the office since we talked last night," I replied, "and the diskette tab prevents writing on all of them. But in addition to dodging the tab protector, either someone had to deliberately issue an erase command, from the PC keyboard or its equivalent, or there had to be some sort of unusual program glitch that sneaks in an erasure once in a while."

"Is that likely?"

"Not very. The most likely thing, I suppose, is that someone is removing the tabs and erasing. It could be the impersonator destroying the pun story, along with thirty others as a sort of smoke screen to hide what he was doing. If that was it, he would have done better to erase the pun story only—probably I wouldn't have noticed. Or he should have made a copy of the disk after he erased the story. Abigail and I talked to Ed Hooper last night, and he pointed out that no one can recover an erased story from a copied disk."

"Has Hooper himself had access to the diskettes?" the Chief asked.

"I'm sure he has, though his name's not in the log," Virg replied.

"He told us he couldn't remember whether he'd used them or not," I said, "and argued that in any case, if he'd done the erasing he'd have made the copy and we wouldn't have found the story. But let me go on. The erasing could also be done by someone who's not altogether familiar with the computer. Maybe he thinks he's trying to erase what's showing on the PC's screen. Maybe he's trying to change the name of a story in the directory, for some reason. I don't know what it could be, but I've seen too many operator mistakes over the years to think such a thing impossible. Let me try out another idea on you."

I went on to explain my theory about strangers and locals, and to raise the possibility that the impersonator might be a professional con man who acquired the deeds after Charlie's death. "Is there a National Register of Con Artists," I asked, "maintained by the FBI or someone? And might they have photos you could show Dubroski?"

"That's an interesting idea," the Chief said. "I'll look into it. I must admit it's a little hard to see how someone from La Aldea could have run Charlie down in Arizona, either by accident or on purpose. But we have to check everything out."

"Did you ask Dubroski what Ryan looks like?" asked Virg.

"Oh, yes, I surely did. He's got snow white hair, and a handlebar mustache. Looks sort of like Mark Twain, according to the banker."

"Nobody around here looks like that," Caroline said. "But it could be a disguise, of course."

"And we have a paper to put to bed, Fred," said Bowman, "with the Ryan story on the front page. If you've finished with your queries, can you leave us to it?"

"I've still got a couple for you. Bill. What was Charlie Ryan like? Was he the kind of fellow who'd be careless with money? We know now he didn't put all those valuable deeds in a bank—at least, not the bank here in La Aldea. But it strikes me as peculiar, him carrying them with him, and figurin' to take them all around the world."

"I see what you mean," Bowman said, thinking for a minute. "Well, I wouldn't say Charlie was careless. He was carrying traveler's checks, not cash, for example. He cleaned out his room before he left—didn't leave any loose ends, that I remember. I don't know how to explain it. Perhaps he put the deeds in a bank in LA. Perhaps he planned to deposit them in a bank somewhere else, like New York." He shrugged. "It's peculiar. Doesn't seem to fit in with what I recollect of his character."

"How'd you come to be rooming with him? Were you old friends?"

"No," Bowman laughed, "no, we hadn't been friends at all. Charlie hadn't had many friends in school. And I don't remember exactly how we got together. I know I'd been living in a small apartment here in town, by myself. I think Charlie had been in one of his own, and we ran into one another somewhere and realized we could move into a bigger place for less rent if we joined forces. But I'm damned if I remember the details. You have any other questions about Aldean antics in the dim past? You want to know what color shirt I wore to work on the last Thursday in November of

1951? Or how many cars drove down Main Street on the average day in 1948? Or are you finished?"

Fred grinned and said he was through, and we all got back to work. My error-checking program had found three mistakes in the forty-five minutes we'd been in Bowman's office, but Sally and Roberta were working on stories, and Virg and Caroline had to have their PC'S back, so I had to postpone further experiments. I got a printout of the errors and sat down in the corner to study them. Maybe I would find a Clue.

CHAPTER 12

Wednesday Afternoon

The morning was to wash my hair and think what to do with the benefit of reasonable doubts. One way or another Chief Fred will see, so there will be some fast moving and more surprise and hurt people. I just had guesses, though proof'll be easy so he's worried maybe gone already, but the world's small and you always hide where you can be found like hide-and-seek.

So I had my breakfast at lunch time at the Cafe with Emil, the others busy working, and he told me all the latest that Arizona and New York and Switzerland and La Aldea could say. He was proud of his Con Man, but of course his very logical tables lead him logically astray, which is the way engineers like to be led. The Scientific Method Recipe for Unwarranted Confidence.

"The paper's out tomorrow so everyone's there hard at work?" said I when he'd finished.

"Virg is still collecting material for the Ryan story," said he. "I'm glad I don't have to work under deadlines like that. I didn't see Martin Neare, but then he pretty much stays out of sight, anyway. George wasn't there, of course. The word is, he's left town."

"Is Chief Fred saying, or quiet?"

"Virg talked to him on the phone late this morning. He's got the FBI interested because the impersonator probably has used Ryan's passport, or has got one under Ryan's name, and also because it turns out they *do* have records on some confidence men. The New York police are helping out, though he didn't say how. I suppose they've arranged for the bank to notify them next time Ryan shows up. And maybe they've got fingerprints off the safe deposit box." He brightened cheerful. "If they found any, maybe they can check them with fingerprints in the FBI'S con-artist file."

"Maybe the Dubroski-banker has a mind's picture," said I.

"Of Ryan, you mean? And is working with a police artist? That's a thought. Maybe the FBI has photos, too, to compare. And what's your theory? You don't have your shoes off this morning. That mean you've got it all worked out?"

Enough food and talk and plenty to do the afternoon with, and Emil always argues logic when I tell what I'm thinking so I got up with my purse ready to go. "It's too cold for bare feet here and now," said I and gave him a kiss and went away him paying the bill.

At the library the file of old *Weekly Aldeans* was missing the issue with the puns, so that was the way I thought. Twenty minutes it took to skim through other old issues to see about travel news. Another twenty in old city directories turned up no Belldicks, but several Hills including a Cynthia. At Valley Realty Mr. Valley was away they didn't know where, left this morning maybe to the lawyer's, but the police had taken the Ryan file so at the police station I waited and found Chief Fred.

"How do you do, Mrs. Lime," said he standing up polite. "I hope this is a social visit, and you haven't come to report a stolen car or a snatched purse."

"No, nothing like that," said I and sat, "but Emil and I enjoy La Aldea, though I suppose it'll change growing the next years. Where did you learn policing?"

"At the Los Angeles Police Academy," said he, "Class of '50. And then working for LAPD. I applied for this job when Jim Kelly retired, in 1964.".

"Two Irish in a row," said I. "Was Chief Kelly thoughtful like Chief O'Leary is?"

"Enough of this blarney now, Mrs. O'Lime," said he laughing at me. "You haven't yet told me why you're here."

"Tom Valley is away but they say the Ryan file is here," said I. "Do you know yet the dates of Ryan banking in New York and Switzerland?"

"We're putting them together," said he eyebrows raised I was glad to hear, "but haven't finished yet. May I ask why you're asking?"

"There isn't an alibi until there's a time and place," said I, "and all the places are so far away."

"Sounds like you think one of our friends, here, may need an excuse," said he puzzled. "I take it you don't agree with your husband's idea about the confidence man?"

"Mrs. 0'Leary's opinion isn't always the same as yours, I'll bet," said I, "and why should an engineer's wife be different from a policeman's?"

"Why, indeed. But if alibis is one side of the story, another side is motives. Which of our local travelers, would you say, is or has been most in need of the ready?"

"You and me and everybody is the easy answer," said I. "More interesting is who've been the big spenders."

"Ah, yes," said he. "I'm having a look at Martin Neare's investment in Chrysler, and the entrepreneurs who put up the cash to finance Ed Hooper's company. It's strange how so much money showed up just about the time Ryan's land was sold."

"Yes it is isn't it, except George Rawlins says he's still a church mouse. Have you heard where George has gone to?" said I, getting up.

"No. Didn't know he was missing."

"Emil ran into him annoyed cursing yesterday after Bill Bowman argued; quit, maybe fired."

"Fired! There's a surprise," said he. "Thanks for mentioning it. I hear Tom Valley and his missus went into town to visit his lawyer, but I'll have to look up old George."

I went out impressed he was doing right things on the track, and walked over to Helen Abernathy invited me right in. "I thought you'd come by again," said she. "Virgil Smith was here this morning with a lot of questions. When you were here yesterday you were anticipating the identification of Charles Ryan's body, and now you want me to tell you more about that young man."

"It's nice to take advantage of a fine memory that's been curiosity provoked," said I.

"Would you like a cup of coffee?" said she, and drinking and talking in the kitchen we went on. "I don't suppose you'd like to explain what it was made you think Charles Ryan was missing?"

"It wasn't Charlie or bodies or missing it was something wrong I didn't know," said I.

"I thought that might be your answer. The trouble is, I wasn't really acquainted with Charles and his generation, and I've already told you everything I remember. His parents kept to themselves. Charles himself was a little strange, and didn't have many friends. There was a girl he went with for a while. She was a nice creature, and felt sorry for him, I think. Nelly Bland, her name was, the daughter of a grocer who was mayor about that time. But they've long since left town, and I have no idea where they might be." Strange no one else remembered Nelly but then Charlie was so quiet he almost disappeared.

"He went on to college must have been a scholar," said I.

"I don't remember his academic record," said she, "but I know he was at UCLA. Bill Bowman was at Berkeley at the same time, and his—Bill's—mother, Shirley, was a good friend of mine. I remember during vacations the boys would josh poor Charles about his going to 'University of California, Hollywood'. Shirley used to tell me about it. But I'm not even sure what it was Charles studied."

"Bill says they roomed shared an apartment together here after graduation, when the fire burned, then up to the time Charlie left La Aldea."

"I didn't remember that, but I can imagine Charles wouldn't have wanted to return to his parents' house after the freedom he found away at college."

"George Rawlins took pictures I don't know where, while Bill and Charlie and Martin Neare were taking courses and coeds in college," said I.

"George lived here in town, but he worked in the City as a free lance, I think the expression is."

"He and Charlie were friends those years of school and lance?"

"I don't really know. They certainly could have been. But George shows such a glum face to the world, he wouldn't have been very good company."

"And Martin Neare didn't get here until the newspaper, after Charlie left around the world. But his home's in Arizona at likely the time the hit-and-run, and now he lives very rich."

Ms. Abernathy looked amazed horrified said, "Good heavens, Abigail! The Neares are a stuffy couple, very proper. Surely you don't . . . I understand Martin has done very well, investing in securities."

"Never a connection you know of Martin and Charlie?"

"Never," said she disgusted my suspicious nature.

"Where was Ed Hooper's college—about the same time, I guess?"

"Yes, the same time. They all graduated from high school the same year. But Ed went east, to MIT or Carnegie Tech or some such. He wouldn't have seen anything of Charles. And besides, he was always a little mean. He would have scorned Charles' shyness and reticence." She looked at me narrow mistrustful, answered a question unasked. "I don't know where Mr. Hooper got the money to start his company. Most of it, I believe, came from outside investors."

"Who was Cynthia Valley before she married, maybe Cynthia Hill?" said I.

"Why, yes," said she surprised. "It was a sort of joke—her married name was Cynthia Hill Valley. But how did you know that?"

"I guessed but couldn't guess was she related to the Hiram Hill that helped Clem Ryan found the town?"

"I have no idea. What on earth . . . why don't you ask her?"

"I will but she's gone right now. Strange Charlie would plan around the world," said I.

"I must agree. I can't imagine where he got the idea. His parents hardly ever left town. But of course young people are often different from their mothers and fathers; and Charles may have had friends at the university who gave him the idea. What is this about, Abigail? Why are you asking all these questions? Surely you don't think anyone here has anything to do with Charles' death?"

Thinking like that was Chief Fred's job I told her, and she huffed indignant, impossible it could be nice neighbors in La Aldea. Our friends can never villains be. Some more talk, then I asked about trips and she told me the travel agent named Mr. Pilgrim's Progresses, and said goodbye. I walked there to find a fat jolly man with his computer in a small two-desk office.

"How-do, ma'am." said he gesturing me at a chair. "May I help you get somewhere? A trip to Timbuktu? An expedition through Arctic blizzards to the Pole? A journey down the Volga River on a raft? You look to me to be a lady ready for adventure. Or do you and your husband just seek a quiet comfortable room in Santa Barbara for the night?"

"Swept off her feet by such dazzling proposals she just wanted to ask some questions," said I, "about Aldean world travelers."

"Ask away, Mrs. Lime," said he. "You are surprised I know your name? You and Mr. Lime are famous already, even before I've sent you off on an action-packed, record-breaking, breath-taking enterprise to some far corner of the whirling earth. The whole town knows the part Mr. Lime played in finding the story, that told of the ring, that led to the teardrop, that named the bones, that revealed the impostor . . ."

". . . That stood in the house that Jack built," said I and he stopped waving his arms.

"Exactly!" said he. "But to answer your question, we have a great many world travelers, not all of whom plan their trips through Mr. Pilgrim. Last year almost fifty of our local families enjoyed the sights of London, Paris, and Rome, and another eighteen or twenty journeyed to the Par East."

Too many to confirm my guess who might be the one, but lots of well-off curious people as I should have expected. We talked of dinner parties and divorces and beauties and boats and unions and universities, and when a customer came in I went out.

"Come again," said he, "and buy a ticket to somewhere," and I waved goodbye and wandered back to the newspaper wondering maybe Emil finished for the day. He wasn't in sight, but downstairs they thought. Caroline was worried at her keyboard and I asked, so she showed me Bill's editorial ready to print.

ARE THINGS AS THEY APPEAR TO BE?

For weeks, the employees of Hooper Electronics have been discussing the advantages of becoming members of the International Union of Electronic Workers. In return for a modest payment of dues, members would be served by a responsible and experienced organization which would represent them in resolving grievances against the company, in improving plant working conditions, in checking unfair or illegal practices, and in insuring that take-home pay and fringe benefits reflect their contributions to the company's success.

What has been the company's reaction to the potential accreditation of IUEW?

"Our workers have no need for a union," says Edward Hooper, company founder and President. "Their wages are near the highest in the industry for comparable work; our plant is clean, well-lit, quiet, brightly-painted, and altogether a delightful place to be; our safety record is exemplary; and our foremen hear and resolve complaints through an informal procedure that works quicker and better than any union-prescribed committee ever could."

The union tells a different story, however. Items:

> . . . Employees complain of boring, repetitive work that strains the eyes and breaks the spirit.
>
> . . . The safety record is far from perfect, as Josanna Nelson can testify. "As I was leaving one night," she said, "I stumbled over something carelessly left in the aisle, fell, and broke my ankle. And the next day I was fired for complaining!"
>
> . . . The company's medical program doesn't cover psychiatric treatment or dental expenses.
>
> . . . Overtime work is assigned with too little advance notice, and no regard for the employees' plans or wishes.

So who are we to believe? Is everything delightful at the Hooper plant, as Mr. Hooper tells us? Or are there dark doings going on despite the "brightly-painted" walls? Should we accept Mr. Hooper's word, or the union's?

An item from this week's news suggests an answer to this question. On Monday afternoon police responded to a call from Hidden Hills, and found Mr. Hooper, partially clothed and badly beaten, in the home of Mrs. Helena Whiteside, 33. John Whiteside, 41, was arrested later and charged with assault. When released on bail, he admitted to reporters that he "banged Hooper around", having come home unexpectedly and found him in bed with his wife. According to Mrs. Whiteside, Hooper met her at a dry cleaners three months ago, and "sweet-talked" her so effectively that she had been seeing him every Monday at noon ever since.

So we have learned a little more about the President of Hooper Electronics, a man who is an elder in his church, a contributor to local charities, a member of the Better Business Bureau and the Chamber of Commerce—a supposed pillar of the community. Everything he says, and all his public actions make him appear to be an honest citizen, devoted to his family and to our city. Mr. Whiteside, however, knows him to be a liar, a debaucher and a cheat.

Perhaps, in voting on unionization, Hooper employees should listen to the Union and to Mr. Whiteside, rather than to their "sweet-talking" company President.

"Very strong words," said I, Caroline looking away guilty but it's not her fault the Editor is looking for scalps.

"You can't be completely impartial, I guess, when you feel so strongly about something," said she. "He believes working people are never treated fairly unless they have a union to back them up."

"Never is a long time and sometimes business is wrong sometimes unions."

"Bill pointed out that my Aldean Annal on Mr. Hooper will serve to tell the other side of the story, and give our readers a more balanced view of things." She sighed. "But of course the news of his affair with Mrs. Whiteside makes the editorial more believable."

"The Union's complaints make the company bad."

"Oh, yes," said Caroline, "it's their business to try to find the bad. But in fact they're wrong. As part of my preparation for the story about Hooper, I spent a full day last week talking to Hooper employees and their families, and almost everyone I met was very happy. Josanna Nelson was fired for being drunk on the job—that's how she happened to fall. She had started drinking at work about a month before, and her foreman and the company had been trying to get her into an AA program. She wouldn't cooperate, and was in fact absolutely stinko the time of the accident. She would have been fired that day if she hadn't broken her ankle." The company was trying to help but couldn't have a drunk at work, and the drunk must have a reason for drinking but wouldn't tell.

"Bill knew Josanna drank her lunch?"

"I told him about it. He said I hadn't heard what she had to say in her own defense, which is true. But I heard the same story from everyone I talked to at the plant, starting with Mr. Hooper himself down to the janitor; and the people at the Emergency Room at the hospital agreed she wasn't at all sober. Ms. Nelson was notorious, and some folks at the plant were actually afraid of her."

"And the boring work and unsafely and medical and overtime?"

"No one I talked to minded the work." Shrugging. "All work is boring sometimes. The plant has a great safety record. And most people would like more overtime work and pay. As for the medical program, there's a management/worker committee that talks about insurance, and no one has ever brought up dental and mental care. The only complaints I ran into were pretty trivial: one fellow felt he should have had a promotion given to a co-worker; three people beefed about the limited selection of food in the cafeteria; a lady thought the coffee breaks should be longer." So the union was puffing a zephyr trying for a hurricane.

"Boswell showed the warts along with the magnificence," said I thinking of the warts we'd seen on Hooper last night.

Caroline laughed wrinkled her nose. "Well, Ed Hooper isn't perfect," said she, "and I show him as I see him. He's sometimes gruff and short-tempered, for one thing, and can rub people the wrong way. But he's aware of his reputation, and compensates by surrounding himself with more gracious people who put up with his bad humor and handle day-to-day company affairs. Then again, he can be perfectly charming when he wants. He was so to me, as he clearly was to Mrs. Whiteside. I think his sourness stems from the days he was growing up, the bright student whose father was a not-very-competent plumber. He wasn't entirely accepted by his friends then, and is still a little suspicious of the world."

"How will the vote go reading your story and Bill's?"

"I don't think most of the people who work out there read the editorials, or even the paper. But whether they do or not, I'm pretty sure the union will lose. Hooper's is a good place to work, and people don't want to pay dues to an organization that really wouldn't do them much good."

"How old is the company?" said I.

"Mr. Hooper set it up in 1983. He was working for Amflight, the big aerospace outfit, and had had this idea for a machine to plot graphs and charts. So he quit and started Hooper Electronics." Long ago Emil had quit a job to start consulting, but that was before we met, and he'd never had worries like Ed Hooper now.

"Besides ideas you need money to buy groceries and socks and transistors and to hire folks," said I.

"I suppose so. I didn't get into that. Some rich people from San Francisco financed him, I believe."

Maybe he had saved a lot, though Caroline didn't know, but the charming irascible brilliant unfaithful man's wife and daughter would be hurt again by the editorial. I said good-bye and walked over to the Cafe past a cloudy sky through a gusty wind. David said Elizabeth was home, so I visited there to warn them the *Weekly Aldean* would speak of lies, debauching, and cheating as if no one had ever before or would ever again mistake. Hooper was nursing bruises out of the hospital now no one knew where, and Florence wrung hands while Elizabeth comforted, and we talked of error guilt apology reform pardon before I got up to say good-bye. Elizabeth took me to the door.

"Thank you for bringing my father's letter," said she. "How did he look?"

"A little banged up, but as cheerful I guess as ever he is. He sent you his love. Did he tell you plans?"

"He said he was going away for a while, and not to worry. He didn't say where. He . . . he said he was sorry I had to know about that Mrs. Whiteside. And that he couldn't explain why he'd done it. Why did he, Mrs. Lime? Where is he? Will he come back to us?"

She was full of questions I couldn't answer, so I reminded her she was someone special no matter who her parents were or why they hurt. She cheered a little, but it's hard to believe in yourself when you're so young knowing the world so little, and I went away glad I was old almost.

CHAPTER 13

Wednesday Afternoon and Evening

It had been a bad afternoon. I read over the error printouts, finally concluding that there must be something wrong with the communication card on Virg's computer. So I interrupted him long enough to remove the card, and drove into Woodland Hills again to get the dealer to test it in one of his PC's. For forty minutes we sent messages around his office without seeing a single error of any kind. The trip had been a complete waste of time, and I climbed into the car and grumbled all the way back to La Aldea.

When I got there they were still hard at work putting the paper to bed, and so I still couldn't claim time on a PC to do some more experiments. I went downstairs to watch the mini laying out pages for the paper, but that was as interesting as watching rain fall on the sidewalk, and there were no examples of missing stories. I thought about our impersonator and wondered what Abigail was up to, and finally gave up and went down to the Cafe for a snack and some friendly conversation with Sadie. She had lots of news, as always, but not much about the Ryan Mystery, as she called it—Chief O'Leary was keeping mum and had cracked down on loose talk by his deputies. However, she told me Ed Hooper had been released from the hospital, but no one knew where he had gone. There had been a three-car accident near the La Aldea freeway exit. Jennifer Able was said to be looking for a job in Los Angeles in case the School Board didn't like the way she lived. George Rawlins had withdrawn his savings from the local bank and either had left the country on a world tour, or was buying a photographic business in Santa Barbara, or was marrying a twenty-year-old model who had posed for him in the nude. Up in Sacramento Sam Ilkins was preparing a bill that would help small towns like La Aldea get state money to finance new schools and other municipal construction. Old Mrs. Hanahan had seen a parrot out in her pepper tree that morning. Abigail had stopped by not long ago, and had gone over to visit with Elizabeth Hooper and her mother.

I broke away from the non-stop late afternoon edition of town talk, and headed back to the newspaper office. I knew Abigail was trying to comfort the ladies, and that I would be in the way if I stopped by at the Hoopers. The mini was still grinding away at layouts, and upstairs Caroline and Virgil and Bowman and Sally were doing the last-minute things that have to be done when the presses start to roll. I cooled my heels for a while, but then Abigail arrived and we went out to dinner—our friends were so busy that none of them could join us.

"Splurge me at The Cloisters," Abigail said as we left, so we got in the car and drove back toward the freeway, then west along an old road that wound through the foothills. It was peaceful and quiet, farms and old homes and big oak trees on rounded hills, and we exchanged stories about how we'd spent our respective days. She told me about Cynthia Valley's maiden name being Hill.

"So she might be related to Hiram Hill," I said, "one of the co-founders of La Aldea? But what difference would that make? You think it might give her and Tom a motive to steal Charlie Ryan's property? Because old Hiram had thought he'd been cheated? That's pretty far-fetched."

"I'm just bringing another fact to the engineer who likes them," she replied, and I gave up.

The restaurant was trying to look like an old English inn, which didn't go either with its name or with its setting, and inside it was dark and gloomy. Obviously the owners didn't appreciate the beauty of the countryside, or perhaps thought that a view of the surrounding hills would encourage people to dally over their desserts and coffee instead of moving on to make room for more customers. But a hostess greeted us with friendly if impersonal enthusiasm and put us in a comfortable corner where we read the menu in candlelight and figured what we would eat.

"Emil," Abigail said when the waitress had taken our order and gone, "the *Aldean* will tell the imposter if we ask."

"The newspaper, you mean?" She nodded. "How is that?"

"Chief Fred has the imposter dates, and the paper has townspeople travel news."

"So you don't buy my theory about the confidence man? Why not?"

"Lots of small things point close to home," she said. "The land's held a long time like somebody knew it was still good; the town's best realtor is hired; the smallest property is sold first; the pun story is missing."

"All those things can be explained," I told her. "A confidence man, once he got the deeds, would visit the town and see the possibilities. He'd be able to hold out a long time, figuring to sell when the property had appreciated and he needed the money to retire on. He probably picked Valley Realty when he was here. And a lot of stories are missing from the diskettes. I don't know exactly how it happened, but they could have been erased accidentally.

"They explained the universe with spheres inside spheres and then gave up when Newton came along," Abigail said. "Here's another straw: the library Weekly Aldean pun is missing."

"The library copy of the paper!" She hadn't mentioned that, and it was an additional coincidence that was hard to explain. "But if you're right, how did it happen that someone local was with Charlie in Arizona when he was killed? Are you saying the imposter accidentally hit him with his car and then discovered he was a neighbor from home? That's a coincidence worse than the small ones you're worried about."

"Maybe he hitched a ride East with a local, maybe Martin Neare living in Arizona hit him by accident, maybe someone here guessed him dead, maybe Cynthia or one of the other Hills or Belldicks are getting even for being cheated, maybe he gave away his property, maybe I don't know. Let's find out what the paper says about who was in New York and Europe, and then see Chief Fred's list of imposter dates from Valley's files and Banker Dubroski."

"And if Bill Bowman or Tom Valley or Chief O'Leary himself or someone happened to be in New York when our Impersonator signed some papers, we report him to the FBI and he's thrown in jail?"

"The impersonator must be worrying Dubroski will recognize his picture."

I could see the point. It was all pretty tenuous and problematic, but then Abigail's reasoning is seldom unassailable, and yet experience has taught me she is sometimes right. Often right. Not always, you understand.

But often. Pretty often. Almost always, in fact. "Do you have a favorite candidate for the villain?" I asked.

"Oh, yes," she said, "but not to tell or you'll tip over the beans." She was pretending I'm transparent and would stare rudely at the guilty party if I knew who it was. "Anyhow, I could be picking the wrong one."

"And should we worry the right one will bang us on the head if he discovers we're onto him?"

"He'll run like a rhino," she replied.

"Away from, not at us, I hope. How do you propose we proceed?"

She explained that she had realized, in skimming through old copies of the *Weekly Aldean* at the library, that the paper *was* pretty thorough in keeping everyone informed of the travels of his neighbors. Both the society and the news columns were full of stories of tours planned and taken, and there were occasional articles devoted to trips made to particular places or to the journeys of particular people. Couldn't the computer look through old issues and point out all such news?

It could, and during and after dinner we talked of how it might be done quickly and efficiently. When we left The Cloisters and headed back to town it was dark, and we drove in thoughtful silence, her head on my shoulder as usual, back to the newspaper office.

There was a light on upstairs, and we found Caroline and Bill straightening up, ready to go home. I explained I wanted some more quiet time to hunt down the last trouble, the intermittent problem in Virgil's PC.

"Would you join us for a drink, Abigail?" Bowman asked. "It won't be any fun watching Emil in pursuit of computer defects, and we can drop you off at your motel afterwards."

"Thanks but I'll keep Emil company, not seeing him much this week," she replied, and so the Bowmans left.

I plugged the card back in Virg's PC and restarted the test which sent messages back and forth between his and Caroline's machines. Since the damned card had worked fine in Woodland Hills, I had to discover whether the problem had disappeared, or was still hanging around. Then we went downstairs to get the archive disks. I sat Abigail down at Sally's PC, called the "Seek" utility program, and showed her how to set up a search.

"You stick one of the old diskettes in," I said, "and type in a list of the words you'd like to find in the archives." I didn't have to explain how to insert a disk—anyone married to a computer expert knows about that. "If the program finds one of the words, it'll put the cursor where it found it and display the story. When you've read it, and copied down the details, you can tell the computer to continue the search by hitting the space bar. When it's looked all through this disk, it'll beep, and you can load another."

She nodded and went to work, and I had a look at Virg's PC. Sure enough, there was another transmission error there, and still none on Caroline's machine. I sat back to think about it. The data was arriving in good shape; no parity error was ever recorded. I knew the trouble wasn't in the parity circuits—I had checked them earlier, by having Caroline's PC send reverse-parity data to Virg. So the problem must be between the register that checked parity, and the PC screen where the messages were displayed. The parity register and some transfer circuits were on the card I had taken to Woodland Hills, and since that card worked there, it must be good. Hold on, now. Let's be cautious. We're dealing here with one of those ghost failures. Maybe the card is really bad, and if I'd tried testing another minute at the dealer's office, the trouble would have appeared. How can I check that out? Easy. Caroline's PC has a communication card, too. I'll switch cards between the two computers. If the trouble is in Virg's card, the errors will then show up in Caroline's machine. In fact, if I'd had any sense I'd have tried that before taking the card into town. I suppose some preoccupation with the Ryan imposter was interfering with my thought processes.

I made the switch and started the test again. While I waited for an error to show, I looked over Abigail's shoulder.

"Find anything?" I asked. She had started looking through 1982 diskettes, since it was August of that year that the imposter had started selling off the property. The words she should look for, we had decided, were Europe, New York, Switzerland, Bowman, Hooper, Meare, Rawlins, Ryan (a long shot), Smith, and Valley.

"Yes, but nothing interesting," she replied, and added, "But I'm still scanning through all the stories figuring I might add to the word list."

"That's a good idea," I said, watching. I noticed she wasn't prepared to record results—was just jotting down notes in an irregular fashion. I found a pad of paper, and set up four columns labeling them "Issue Date", "Person", "Travel Dates", and "Destination."

"Use this to list what you find," I said, showing her the pad, "and record the issue date of the paper even if you don't find anything useful, so we'll know we checked it."

She looked at my columns, smiled up at me, and pulled my necktie so my head came down where she could kiss me. Then she wrote down the date of the first diskette she'd checked, copied her irregular notes onto my orderly form, and went on scanning.

I returned to Virg's machine and found two problems recorded since I had switched cards, and still no trouble on Caroline's PC. Okay. So the trouble wasn't in the card I'd switched—it was something else in Virg's PC. Something in the small buffer where characters were held until the program could use them. Could I check out that buffer? Aha! Yes, I could, because the PC actually had provision for two buffer cards, and we were only using one. I referred to the manual, and discovered those cards should occupy positions five and six. Took the cover off the PC, found the buffer card in slot five, and moved it to six. Replaced the cover and started the test again.

Abigail was scanning through her fourth diskette. "I've found some new words: Newark and La Guardia and Kennedy International," she said. "Ed and Florence Hooper flew La Guardia early February for an electronics convention, and the paper didn't say 'New York'."

"Did you go back and have the PC check those first diskettes for the three airports?" I asked.

"Maybe later if there's no success," she said. I suggested she list the words she was seeking, so if she added more as the evening progressed she would have a record of what she might have missed, and she nodded and wrote them at the top of the page.

Back at Virg's machine I found no errors! That was promising, though not conclusive. But I was optimistic. I let the test continue while I turned on the spare PC, made myself a chart like the one I had prepared for Abigail, and started looking through the 1983 archive diskettes for travel news.

After a while I realized it was taking about five minutes to search through a disk. So it'd take four hours to handle a whole year, and we had more than five years to go. We also had five PC'S, and they could all work at the same time, each on a different year. I went into Bowman's office and started his machine searching the first 1984 diskette. Then I had another look at Virg's. Still no troubles. So I assumed I'd located the failure in his PC, and could use it and Caroline's to search two more years. I interrupted Abigail, and explained what I was doing.

CHAPTER 14

Wednesday Evening
and Thursday Morning

The computer's a faceless genius at doing what you want and no more, so this was just the job for it. It dug out travelers, and we wrote down their names dates places and told it to find more. For a while I went on skimming scanning every issue in 1982, and added Connecticut, Jersey, and Manhattan to the list of things to look for while Emil got the other four computers looking. Then we were as busy as the Ice cream vendor with his helper out sick at noon on a sunny Independence Day at the amusement park next to the roller coaster, going from machine to machine as they found trips. But the hours passed and the evidence piled up.

Mr. Pilgrim was right saying surprising how many local folks visited the Big City and Europe. Almost everyone on our list had crossed the Atlantic the last five years, and all were in New York at least once or several times. Others not on the list too, like Chief Fred and Roberta Orr and Evan Jitney and Elmer Wilkins the Fire Chief. It was a rare issue that didn't brag on some resident away, and by three a.m. we were pooped with over 200 names and dates copied out in Emil's tidy columns. When the last diskette of the last year rolled to a stop we shut down put away locked up and headed for the motel. I brushed my teeth over pages and saw what Chief Fred would find and wasn't surprised. And we went to bed curled together after a tired kiss.

We slept like December bears and didn't wake 'till ten. By eleven-thirty we'd packed our bags, checked out saying goodbye to manager Jitney, and did the drug store to make a copy of the notes. We stopped by the police station. Chief Fred was in.

"Abigail thought you'd be interested in Aldean travelers," said Emil handing the list over, "and so last night we had the computers look through old copies of the paper. These are the results, if you want them."

The Chief shuffled through them blunt-fingered, then looked up at us. "Very useful," said he, "very useful indeed. I've talked to Jack Pilgrim, the local travel agent, but he's a little reluctant to let us go through his records without permission from his customers, and I was trying to decide whether to get the City Attorney's help, or what. I hadn't thought of trying to dig stuff out of the newspaper."

"The paper like Sadie even isn't a perfect reporter," said I, "and so some trips were taken but aren't here. And there are some as private as shadows, who fade and flit and don't like their travels known. But likely you'll find what you want."

"We'll get right to it." He picked up the phone and someone was to send someone else to him. "Thanks very much for the help. Did it take long?"

"We were up 'till the early hours," Emil confessed. "How long will it be before you can come to some conclusion?"

"I'd guess a couple of hours," said Chief Fred. "I'll let you know what we learn. Where will you be?"

Emil said we'd have breakfast at the Cafe, then go on over to the *Aldean* office, and we left hungry ready to eat.

"Good mornin'," said Sadie and sat us down and poured. Tom Valley and his buddies sat their special table, and he waved smiled at us. "You've seen the paper, have you?" said Sadie. "Charlie Ryan dead for years, and Bill Bowman rakin' Ed Hooper over the coals, the poor sinner. Young David is furious with his father." She noticed we looked around for the young man, and added, "Elizabeth came in with a long face, and I told him to take the mornin' off and cheer her up. I expect they're in the park. What'll you have?"

I ordered a short feed and Emil saw I was hurrying and did the same. Sadie was a busy busboy, with David away, and most of the time her arms covered with plates. When she unloaded our breakfast from wrist and elbow, I asked whether anyone'd heard from George.

"Nope," said she, "not a thing. They say he went to New York, and is snappin' pictures of tourists out by the Statue of Liberty. But I think he's just off somewhere havin' a quiet drunk, and will show in a day or two, apologize to Bill, and go back to work again." And away she went to deliver the rest of her burden.

In twenty minutes we'd finished and paid the piper and farewelled Sadie, and found the two young lovers sitting in the park. Elizabeth saw us coming, and she took David's hand and brought it and him to us.

"Did you see the paper?" said David.

"Why did he do it, Mrs. Lime?" said Elizabeth. "Why did he see that woman, and lie to mother and me?" I'd tried to answer that question when we talked before, but now the editorial had her worried again like a kitten with a football rolled at her.

"You still haven't seen him?"

"No. He hasn't come home or called, and I guess no one knows where he is."

"Let's go sit," said I and we headed for benches in the shade. The park was a good place to talk where the trees and squirrels and fish in a small pond helped you accept humans by not seeing them. "He'll tell you about the woman some day," said I, "but maybe not soon. Maybe he's ashamed, of her and of the sneaking. But we all cheat sometimes, like little kids telling ourselves it's for the best and no one will find out."

"Grown people shouldn't lie," said she, her head shaking insisting stubborn.

"Did your father lie? Really? Did he tell you he wasn't seeing Mrs. Whiteside?"

"Of course not. We didn't even know about her. He lied just by pretending one thing and doing another. By keeping quiet about his affair." At "affair" she scowled frowning, didn't like the word or the idea or her father having one.

"We all lie sometimes by keeping quiet. I'll bet the two of you are guilty as your father. Have you told your parents everything about yourselves? About all the different things you've read, for example? About the grass you tried and the booze you sipped? About the times you broke the family rules and hitchhiked, or drove without your seatbelts? About necking in the car evenings up on the hill?" They looked at one another more than a little guilty. "And of course you and David would have been happier if his father hadn't mentioned your Dad's affair in his editorial. You'd have preferred his lying by silence."

They had to stop and think about that a minute, two calves coming to a fence, and then they turned and David said, "It wasn't just his bringing it up. It was the other things. He said we couldn't believe anything Mr. Hooper said, just because of that Mrs. Whiteside. Just because he lied about one thing, doesn't mean he lies about everything!"

"That's absolutely right, David," said I, "and I think your father was wrong with that argument. But parents are people like everybody else and their kids shouldn't be surprised. If they make mistakes, they still love their children more than themselves," hoping I was right, "so we have to forgive them."

"Not when they hurt people without even caring," said David, thinking of course his father hurt him and his mother as well as Elizabeth.

"Even then," said I. "Remember the times they've forgiven you when you've been wrong. And something else I want you both to remember. You've found father faults. But you haven't found them all. As time goes by, others will turn up, and you're going to have to keep your pardoning machines in good repair, ready to use again and probably again."

"Nothing can be worse than what my father's done already," said Elizabeth. "He's shamed us in front of the whole world."

"It's his own face that's red, not yours. You've done nothing to be ashamed of. You can feel uncomfortable for him, if you like, but your own head should be held up. No one in town says his peccadilloes are yours."

"They feel sorry for me," said she.

"Maybe so, but that should make you feel good, not bad. They're sympathetic, knowing how you must be hurt. Some are maybe guilty thinking on their own secrets, and how their families and friends would suffer if the world knew." I got up, holding Emil's hand. "Emil's finished curing the computers, and we'll be heading home today. You are two fine kids, and don't forget it. Cheer up. And remember about father faults: there'll be others, so practice up on being a forgiver."

"In other words," said Emil, "she's telling you to cheer up—the worst is yet to come."

Emil didn't know he'd be right so soon, but he brought a smile to two handsome glum faces, and they said thanks and bid us good-bye and we went off to the paper.

Caroline and Virgil were there fussing odds and ends, both dressed in warm old clothes. "Where's Bill?" said Emil. "I want to give him a final report."

"He's gone ahead, out to the marina to get the Faraway ready," said Caroline. "We're sailing to the islands today."

Emil was surprised, but said, "Well, I had hoped to see him again, but I guess it doesn't matter. Tell him I think I got everything straightened out. Virg's machine has a bad communication slot, but I've switched to the spare, and you can have the bad one fixed next time a serviceman comes out. I'll send on a complete report and bill next week." He fished into his pocket. "Here's the office key. I won't be needing it again."

Caroline took the key and said, "That sounds just fine, Emil. I know Bill will be pleased. And now you're headed for home? Santa Monica, is it?"

"That's right," said I. "But we're not leaving traveling just yet. We'll mosey the town here for a while say good-bye to acquaintance friends. When d'you think you'll leave drive to the marina?"

"In about an hour, I'd guess. We have a little more to take care of here."

"Then let's not goodbye now," said I. "We'll stop by here again before we leave town. I'm still hoping to find out the dragon that swallowed up George. You haven't heard from him or where he is or what he's doing?"

"No," said she, "not a word. He hasn't called you, has he, Virg?"

"Nope. But I think he has to come back. He's left hundreds of negatives here in the files. Maybe he'll come in this weekend while we're away. Then he won't have to confront Bill."

"We'll be off to do our moseying, then," said I. "If anyone calls while we walk, take a message say we'll be back soon."

We left, and Emil looked at me eyebrows raised to know what we'd do next. I took him down Main Street stopping at the shops to introduce my charming engineer husband and visit a while, spending time and a little money on this and that here and there. We were coming out of the florist when a police car passing stopped sudden and the officer got out to say Chief Fred would like to see us.

"The Chief told me you'd be downtown somewhere, ma'am," holding the car door for us, "and sure enough, I found you in my first pass along Main."

At the Chief's office we sat and he began, "Your notes did the trick. Did you guess the name of the guilty party?"

"Bill Bowman," said I.

CHAPTER 15

Thursday Morning

I looked at her and I suppose my jaw was hanging down, but she just looked back with the grave expression she reserves for bad times. And the Chief agreed with her.

"That's right," he said. "It's all circumstantial evidence, but the New York police found fingerprints on the safe deposit box, and we'll be able to prove it when they get Bowman's prints. Also, I imagine that Dubroski will recognize his picture, even if Bowman's been wearing a disguise when he visits the bank."

"Bowman!" I said. "You've got to be kidding! Are you saying he went on that trip with Ryan in fifty-two, and murdered him in Arizona? That's crazy. Bill's not a murderer. And if he was, why would he kill Ryan out there? Why not closer to home?"

"Well, I've been thinking about it since we saw how his trips the last few years to New York and Europe fit in with the impostor's visits, and I think the answer is, no one murdered Ryan. He was killed in a hit-and-run accident by some stranger we'll never find."

"Then how did Bowman get the deeds and papers?"

"Maybe Ryan gave them to him before he left," the Chief said. "Remember, they were rooming together. Suppose Ryan asked Bowman to hold them for him, or to open a safe deposit box and put them away. Or suppose he just left them in a box or a drawer in their apartment, figuring he'd retrieve them when he got back. He was only going to be gone a year, remember."

"And when Bill didn't hear from him that whole year," Abigail said, "and another few years passed with not a word and no return, Bill guessed him dead. He needed money for newspaper starting in fifty-six and sold that first land, thinking if Charlie came back they were friends and it would be a loan. And by eighty-two it was all his he had held it so long, and he started selling the rest for a Swiss bank and retiring."

I could see how that might all fit together, even if I didn't believe it of Bowman. "Let's see what Bill says. Have you tried to reach him at the marina?"

"Yes, but he hasn't arrived."

"He'll never arrive," Abigail said. "He's on his way somewhere else right now, and he's not Bill Bowman anymore and won't ever be."

"I think she's right. Emil," the Chief said. "Bowman must have seen he was trapped as soon as Virg found the pun story and we realized Ryan was dead. He's been making preparations for years. He's just become someone else—the same someone else who has all the money in the Swiss bank—and hopes to make his way to Europe. He figures he can find some pleasant place to retire, and live the rest of his life very comfortably. He hasn't got away yet, though."

"But maybe you're both wrong," I argued. "Maybe he's detoured somewhere on his way to the marina. Maybe your fingerprints and photo won't match."

"Maybe so," the Chief said. "I sent the prints and picture to New York half an hour ago by wire, and should have an answer before too long. Meanwhile, I've got the

Sheriff and the LA Police looking for Bill's car. No one's seen it yet."

"It was when that story came out," Abigail said, "the one with the governor finding the body in Arizona. It was only then he was sure Charlie would never return. But the story scared him as much as it cheered him, because the ring told him it was Charlie but someone here might remember the ring or old Somers Grant's article and know Ryan was dead that the jig was up. So he got rid of the pun story in the computer and the library."

"The library?" the Chief asked.

"They have old copies of the *Weekly Aldean* there but not the old copy with Mr. Grant's puns."

Bowman had said he hadn't read the pun story, but of course if he was the villain, he was lying. I didn't want to believe it, but maybe that was because I had liked him, on the whole. Or maybe it was because Abigail had seen it and I hadn't. I suddenly realized her remarks that morning about the importance of forgiving errant fathers had been aimed at David as much as at Elizabeth. "How is David going to take this?" I asked. "And Caroline?" But it was as much to myself as to Abigail and the Chief.

"Virgil and Elizabeth will be glad to comfort." Abigail said. "And Bill must have left somewhere a story for Caroline to find so he could explain and she would know." She got up and headed for the door.

"Hold on a minute, Mrs. Lime," the Chief said. "You're not going to tell Caroline yet, are you? There's still a chance I could be wrong. I don't want her to know unless the New York police tell me those are indeed Bill's prints on the safe deposit box."

"We told her we'd be back to say good-bye," Abigail said, "and that's what we'll be doing. But we'll also look for the message. If we don't find a letter and you haven't heard from New York, she and Virgil will soon be on their way out to the marina they think to meet Bill."

The Chief nodded, and we headed back to the newspaper. As we walked, Abigail said, "It's funny Bill didn't leave a message thanking the stalwart and efficient consultant or something."

"That'd have been the last thing he'd think of, if he was worrying about getting away before he was found out."

"But you could ask Caroline to look," my devious wife said, and I realized what she wanted.

Virgil and Caroline were still there, sitting at their desks. Evidently they had cleaned up the last of their work and were waiting for us.

"We were wondering what had become of you," Caroline said. "Have you finished your good-byes? We still haven't heard from George."

"Yes," I said. "Abigail introduced me to several people so we could say goodbye to them. And I was wondering: did you run across a note from Bill to me? He might have left one, knowing we'd be going home today."

"We haven't really looked. I should think he would have put it on my desk, if he'd written one." She thought for a moment. "Maybe he left it on his own desk."

The four of us trooped into Bowman's office and looked around. There was no envelope or letter in sight, and Caroline hesitated, then opened a desk drawer. "I don't see anything," she said.

"Probably he figured on talking to you on the phone," Virg said. "There wasn't any particular reason he should have left you a note, was there?"

"No," I said. "I was just curious." A possibility had occurred to me, and I walked over to his PC and switched it on. "Does he ever leave messages on his computer?" I asked.

Caroline smiled. "Never," she said. "That's something only a computer consultant would think of."

"I have to disagree," I told her. "Look at this." The other three gathered around the PC and looked at the screen.

Dearest Caroline-In the bottom right-hand drawer of my desk, under the stack of file folders, you'll find a diskette. Please put it in drive B, and then hit the carriage return button. Maybe you'll want to read what it says in private . . .

Caroline frowned. "Wouldn't you know," she said. "He's always trying something new." She sat in Bowman's chair, fished around in the bottom right drawer, and came up with a disk. "Maybe he wants me to tell you something?"

"It says a private message," Abigail said, "so we'll go and you read and come and tell us about it." She motioned to Virg and me, and we left and shut the door while Caroline was installing the disk.

"What's that all about?" Virg asked. "It's a strange way to leave a message."

It occurred to me it was a good way if you didn't want a written record that could be used in court, but I didn't say anything.

"I think it's going to be bad news and she's going to need sympathy, Virgil," Abigail said as we sat down to wait.

"Bad news? What do you mean, bad news? What kind of bad news?" Virg was beginning to worry, and got up as if to go back into Bowman's office. I suddenly realized his feelings for Caroline were more than those any young man has for a pretty woman. Evidently Abigail had figured that out long ago.

"Let's sit down and wait and we'll find out," she said, and Virg subsided back into his chair. "It'll be the kind of bad news the prospector gets finding when he wakes in the morning that his burro Juliet has wandered away, but in the end it'll be good 'cause he'll go off looking for her and find the lost mines of the El Dorado."

It was an answer that hardly satisfied Virg, but he couldn't persuade my wife to say anything more, and finally we waited in silence, each thinking worried thoughts. Ten minutes passed before the door opened. Caroline was standing there, very pale. If I'd had any doubts about Bowman's guilt, I discarded them right then. Abigail went to her.

"Are you all right?" she said. "Come sit down and tell us."

Caroline sat at her desk, Abigail holding her hand, and looked around, dazed. "I don't understand," she said. "I can't believe it."

"What is it, Caroline? Are you feeling okay?" Virg was standing in front of her, clenching his fists, obviously ready to defend her but not knowing what from.

"He's gone. Bill's gone. He says I won't see him again. He's going to disappear. He was the one who sold Ryan's property." She looked at Abigail. "But he didn't kill him," she said. "He just sold it when he realized Ryan must be dead. How could he . . . What am I going to do? What will happen to him?" Tears came then, and she rubbed her cheek with the back of her hand. Virg stood next to her thunderstruck, his mouth open, not believing what he'd heard.

"First of all," I said, "you should know that O'Leary caught on this morning. He's looking for Bill, though as of half-an-hour ago he hadn't found him. The point is, if Bill hadn't left, he'd be facing jail right now."

"There's a good chance he won't be found," Abigail said. "Likely he's had a plan a long time how to end Bill Bowman and become Mr. Freshbody, like a flying fish folding his fins and falling back into the sea."

"He's been planning this all along? To leave me?"

"Since the article last year about the body in Arizona," Abigail said. "That's what's the hardest to see and believe." There were tears in her own eyes now. "I'm afraid you didn't know him as well as you thought you did, but then remember everybody thought wrong seeing him the way he saw himself not how he really was. So we'll all have to revise our picture of Bill, and it'll be hardest for you of course but once done that's the worst and you'll be all right."

"I don't believe it," Virg said. "Bill wouldn't think of leaving you, Caroline. There must be some mistake."

She smiled at him a little, feeling better because he was so obviously worried. "That's what I thought," she said, "but I'm afraid it's no mistake. His letter was apologetic, but very clear. He's gone." She was bearing up remarkably well.

"What else did the letter say?" I asked.

"Well, he told me . . . But why don't you read it for yourselves." She got up, and led us back to Bowman's office. "It wasn't a sentimental, or romantic letter. There's no reason you shouldn't see it. How can we get it back. Emil?"

Bowman's PC was still on, with nothing showing on the screen but the cursor. I sat at the keyboard. The message to Caroline had appeared when we first turned on the computer, and that's when every PC calls its automatic batch program. So I typed the name of that program, and sure enough got the "Dearest Caroline" message that asked her to find the diskette. The disk was still in place, so I hit the ENTER button. There was a pause, then the words

"File does not exist" showed up on the screen. I looked at the directory of the B disk drive, and it was blank; the diskette Caroline had got from the drawer, the one that had contained the letter, had been erased. I looked inside the automatic batch program, and found the "Dearest Caroline" message, followed by a call to display a document stored on disk B—the letter Caroline had read, obviously—followed by a command that would wipe out the letter and anything else on that disk.

"When you'd finished reading," I said to Caroline, "did you tell the computer to format the diskette in drive B?"

She looked a little perplexed. "Yes, I think so. It asked me if it was okay."

I nodded. "What's happened is, Bill set up a letter that could only be read once. It's been destroyed, now." I took the disk out, and put it in its protective sleeve. "We ought to give it to the Chief, but I don't think anyone can retrieve it, after the disk has been formatted. You'll just have to tell us what you remember, Caroline."

She and Abigail and Virg had taken seats while I was working at the PC, and she looked around the room a minute, gathering her thoughts. "He said it just happened," she began. "Ryan had gone, saying he would write, and leaving his papers, including the deeds and his birth certificate, in a box. Bill got that single postcard from Barstow or somewhere, and then heard nothing more—nothing at all. He began to wonder whether something had gone wrong, but what could he do? Charlie had no family. There was no one he could notify, no one else was worried. He mostly forgot about it."

As Caroline continued it was clear that what Chief O'Leary had said was right on track. Bowman needed money to start the paper. He figured probably Charlie was dead. He looked through the papers carefully for the first time, hoping to find a will, but there was nothing like that.

"Bill said he had been Charlie's best friend, actually his only friend, and was sure that if Charlie had written a will, he'd have been the beneficiary. So by rights, the property belonged to him, and he decided to sell part of it so as to be able to finance the *Weekly Aldean*." She looked around the office again, a bewildered sort of expression on her face, thinking, I suppose, of how many hours Bill had spent here and how easily he had left the newspaper, and her. I wondered what she thought of his arguing 'by rights, the property belongs to me'. It certainly told us something about Bowman: that he felt there was some kind of 'true' law on his side, and that it exonerated him from charges of theft, forgery, and whatever else he'd done.

"So he went back east and established himself somehow as Charles Ryan," she went on. "He mentioned that he used Charlie's birth certificate to get a passport in Ryan's name, and he introduced himself at the DuPair bank, and said he was born in La Aldea but lived in Europe and wanted to sell a piece of property. I can't imagine how he fooled them, though I know he'd been in Europe once himself when he was a student, or just after he was out of college. He wrote a letter to Tom Valley authorizing the sale and saying the bank would handle the paperwork, and then came on home.

"He made his plans for the paper, and waited. When Tom sold the lot, he made another trip to New York, signed the deeds and things, and brought back enough money to buy a cheap press and get the paper going. He said he pretended the money was a loan from a friend of his father's."

"That must have been the $20,000 Dubrosky mentioned," I said. "I'll bet he withdrew it in cash. If he'd got a check, the bank would wonder why it was cashed out in California, when the so-called 'Ryan' said he lived in Europe."

"Bill didn't say anything about that. Anyhow, the paper was a success, and the years went by. He married, and David was born, and in 1982 he started selling the rest of the property. He wanted to retire, he said, and live comfortably. Anyhow, he divorced David's mother, and we were married in '84. We spent our honeymoon in Europe—I suppose when we were in Geneva he stopped at that Swiss bank where he'd deposited the money from the sales. He says he was going to tell me a distant relative had left him a fortune, and that we'd live somewhere in Greece.

"But then the news came out about Ryan's death this week, and he saw it wasn't going to work. He wouldn't give up the money, he said, so he'd have to run. And he couldn't ask me to run with him." She had a strange expression on her face. "I wonder what I would have done, if he'd asked. And that was it. He ended just by saying good-bye, and that he'd always remember me." I thought of the utter impossibility of my leaving Abigail, of the desolation I'd feel if anything happened to her, and my waning sympathy for Bowman faded into the fogs of disgust.

"He didn't say anything about a power of attorney, or any legal documents?" I asked.

She looked doubtful. "No. Why should he have?"

"Well, there's your home, and the newspaper," I said, "and I imagine they're both in his name. If the police don't catch up with him—if he just disappears—that property will be in a sort of limbo, I think. It won't be yours, and if he doesn't exist, it won't be his. I thought he might have deeded it over to you, or something."

Just then the phone rang, and Caroline picked it up and said hello. She listened, and handed it to me. "It's the Chief," she said.

Fred told me they had already heard from New York, and that the prints matched; they had absolute proof Bowman was the imposter. I described the letter Caroline had received, and he asked to speak to her again. When they'd finished, she hung up and said, "He'll be right over, Emil. He wants to see the disk, and I told him he could look through Bill's office." She got up. "He also said he hadn't been able to reach Jill, David's mother, and that he wondered if I'd tell David right away. He says the news will soon be out—he can't keep it quiet—and that he thought it'd be better David hears it first from me than from some tattletale. Would you come with me, Abigail, and help me break it to him?"

When the ladies left, Virg said, "She's amazing, isn't she. A blow like that would put most women into hysterics, and she's hurrying out to help David."

"It's a good sign, I'd say. Apparently her devotion to Bowman isn't all that strong."

Virg was indignant. "That's not true!" he said. They were very close. I just can't imagine why he'd abandon her. He must be out of his mind."

"It would have been tough for him to stay. He'd have to give up all the money. He'd probably be charged with forgery, and obtaining a passport under a false name, and he might even be tried for murder. And he could avoid all that trouble just by disappearing."

"And by giving up Caroline," said Virg.

"If you were he, would you have stayed, and had her visiting you at prison on weekends?"

"I'd never have sold the property. He had Caroline. What other riches would anybody want?"

Before I could respond to that romantic statement, we heard footsteps on the stairs and the Chief rolled in followed by a deputy.

"What's the news?" I asked. "Have you found Bowman?"

"Not yet. What did he say to Caroline?"

We told him what we remembered, and I gave him the disk. He and the deputy started a systematic search of Bowman's office, looking for some sort of clue as to where the fugitive might have gone. They did a careful job, and left everything as they found it. In a little less than an hour they were nearly through but had learned nothing, and Caroline and Abigail returned.

"Did you see David?" I asked.

"Yes," Caroline said. "He and Elizabeth were in the park, and we told them about Bill. He took it pretty well."

"The thunderbolt struck," Abigail added, "but as soon as his ears stopped ringing he said he wasn't surprised a man who left one family would leave another, a man that'd lie in editorials would lie in real life. It was Elizabeth's turn to cheer *him* up, and we helped and then finally his mother Jill came and the three of them went off. He'll be all right, but there'll be some nights of tears and no sleep, private out of sight, before he'll accept the world again. Have you found anything that'll give Caroline and Jill and David any comfort or cash?"

"Not yet," replied the Chief. "And we haven't found anything pointing to where he's gone. Do you have any ideas, Caroline? Did he ever say anything that might give you a clue?"

"Don't answer, Caroline," said Virg. "You have no right to ask her that, Fred—to try to make her put her husband in prison."

"It's all right, Virg. I have no idea where he could have gone. He never said or did anything that hinted at what he was planning."

The Chief asked her to repeat what Bowman had said on the disk, and when she was about half-way through a call came in saying that the LA Police had found Bill's car downtown, but that there was no sign of its owner.

"He's probably on a plane to Europe by now," I said.

"Or on a bus, or a train, or in a car he's just bought under his new name," the Chief added, "or even in a car he bought weeks or months ago, and has had stored away. I'm beginning to have the feeling we're not going to find him."

At this further reminder that her husband had been planning a disappearance while apparently living an ordinary life with her, Caroline gave 'way to tears again. She didn't shudder, or cry out. She simply turned away. Abigail took her hand, and said, "He's not a Jessie James. He's just a Dwight Eisenhower or a John Madden or a Grace Kelly that ends one kind of life for a new better one like dying and going to heaven."

John Madden! Where had Abigail heard about John Madden? She's never watched a football game in her life. But then she's always surprising me. At any rate, Caroline was cheered to hear Abigail connect her husband with the accomplished and notable, and to realize she'd rather have him disappear than confront the Angel Gabriel. She recovered her self-possession and continued her account of what he had said on the diskette. The Chief had some questions, and then returned to his office, leaving us to comfort Caroline and to try to understand what had happened.

By now word of Bowman's defection had reached the town, and we began to get telephone calls, and even visits from friends and from *Aldean* employees who couldn't believe the news. Virg handled them, confirming the facts, assuring everyone that the paper would continue to be published as before, and shooing people away from Caroline. Finally he suggested we adjourn to his apartment, where it was less likely we'd be bothered, and where he could fix us a lunch.

He had a very modest couple of rooms—a small kitchen and a sitting room furnished with a convertible sofa, second-hands, and discards—not far from the office. Caroline had evidently not seen it before, and looked around a little dismayed. Virg didn't notice. He took his phone off the hook and then went into the kitchen. In a minute he returned to say he could offer cheese or tuna sandwiches, or could go down to the market and buy the fixings for something more exotic. We settled on what he had, and were soon picnicking in comfortable silence. A knock on the door interrupted us.

"Who is it?" said Virg.

"Open up, Virg," came a voice. "It's me. Your ol' drinkin' and whorin' buddy, George."

Virg looked at Caroline, who nodded, and he unlocked and opened the door. George came in, took us all in at a glance, and immediately went to Caroline. "It was a lie," he said to her. "Drinkin', yes. Whorin', no. Not Virg. How are you doing, honey?"

"About as well as can be expected," she replied. "But where have you been?"

"That's a long and interesting story," he said, "and one you might not have believed yesterday. Hows about me getting one of them sandwiches, Virg?"

Virg grinned and went into the kitchen, and George turned to us. "The technological Emil and the redoubtable Abigail," he said. "Look at all the woes you've brought down on us."

"George!" Caroline was provoked. "Don't be silly."

"Well, If Emil here hadn't dug up the buried story . . ."

"If Bill hadn't hired Emil," Virg said, handing George a sandwich and a mug of beer, "he wouldn't have been here to dig. Blame it on Bill."

"I find it hard to argue with you on that point, my friend," George said. Then turning to Caroline, "A remarkable man, your erstwhile husband. Thoughtful, reasonable, intellectual, liberal, understanding, warm-hearted, kind . . . I've wandered the town the past hour, looking at faces and hearing his paeans rung." He took a large swig of beer. "Or mebbie I mean sung."

"He's not erstwhile," Caroline argued. "We're still married."

"Erstwhile," George repeated, "and both rung and sung. People first find it hard to believe. They lift their shoulders and widen their eyes and squinch up their faces and say, 'He was all for saving the whales, and campaigned for money for Africa's starving children. He was against discrimination and for disarmament. How could such a fella be a thief?'" He frowned, and turned again to Caroline. "Begging your pardon, ma'am."

"Lay off, George," Virg said. "Caroline doesn't need that kind of crap."

"It's all right," Caroline put in. "I think it's better for me to talk about it and hear about it. What else are people saying?"

"Everybody wishes you well. But as they keep reviewing it in their minds' eyes, folks remember Ed Hooper's troubles, and begin to feel sad and sorry. All their heroes have clay feet. This morning they read Bill's editorial on Ed's transgressions, and on the same day they discover the editorialist is guilty of even worse shenanigans. La Aldea seems to be a hypocrite's paradise."

"You're one of the worst, yourself," Abigail said. "Everybody's caught on to your game long ago, acting the lion and being the lamb."

"Horsefeathers!" George said. "I plead guilty to pretending, but I'm acting the lion, living the hellhound. Meanwhile, I blench and sorrow listening to my lyin' neighbors. There's Frank Orr, who can't work, and collects disability pay for his bad back, but is always healthy when it's time for a pickup game of football or basketball down at the park. There's Mary-Jane Orange, the churchgoing shoplifter who stays out of jail only because her husband keeps payin' off all the local merchants. There's plumber Sam Selig, who was plumb outraged at Bill's caper, but himself dodges taxes by fixin' your pipes on a cash-only basis."

"They all figure they're too smart ever to get caught," I said.

Abigail was shaking her head. "They're like all the rest of us, knowing what we do is right for that's why we do it. Ed Hooper figured success in business allowed a little success in seduction, and Bill Bowman sold property that was his because Charlie Ryan would have left it in his will. For sure Mr. Orr thinks himself sick, and Mrs. Orange thinks she's poor, and Mr. Selig thinks he pays too many taxes already."

"Mebbie so," George said. "But our friend and ex-boss wins all the prizes. He was a great one for talking of the good of mankind; but when it came to action, he concentrated on the good of Bill Bowman."

"Hold on now, George," Virg said. "That's not fair at all. Bill was a good citizen in every way. I'm sure he never cheated on his taxes or his marriage, and certainly his conduct was consistent with his beliefs."

"Well, I'll grant you one thing: so far as I know, he never killed a whale. But the rest of his glib goodness is suspect, as far as I'm concerned. Take discrimination, for example. How many blacks, Orientals, Hispanics, and Jews do you find on the staff of his newspaper?"

There was a moment of silence, and Caroline said, "None. But there aren't many who live in La Aldea; and none that I know of have ever looked for a job with us."

"There have been applicants now and again," George said, "and there's no doubt Bill always had good reasons why they weren't qualified. So let me take another subject: charity. Us public-spirited *Weekly Aldean* employees have always signed up for a charitable deduction from our paychecks, right? But I happen to know Bill never did. Of course, those deductions appear every year on the forms we send Uncle Sam in April. Do you mind saying, Caroline, whether Bill made up for his paycheck parsimony with big contributions to his favorite charities?"

Caroline blushed a bit and said, "Actually, mine were the only ones. Bill always said his contribution was the time and effort he took to convince and motivate everyone else to be charitable."

"An admirable contribution, I'm sure," George said. "Let me try something else. He was always cussin' out folks who he said made our highways unsafe, and he came on strong for the 55-mile speed limit, and seat belts, and big trouble for drunk drivers. But we've all driven with him. We've all seen him use the ol' radar detector. Did he obey the speed limit law? No. Ever wear a seat belt? No. Ever drive while under the influence? Yes."

"Come on, now, George," Virg said. "That's all pretty picayune stuff. And it wasn't often he drove a little inebriated."

"But as he pointed out from his editorial pulpit," George replied, "it only takes once to kill or cripple somebody. Picayune? Hell, I'll go along with you there. Life is just one damned picayune thing after another. Mebbie that's one of the things that was wrong with the boss. He was only interested in the big picture, the universal truths. He couldn't be bothered with the details."

"Caroline mentioned his editorial on Ed Hooper's plant and unions, Bill sitting in his office mind closed not seeing for himself what was going on," Abigail said, and Caroline nodded—a little sadly, I thought.

"Ah, yes," George said. "Unions. That brings me to my last story. Did Bill tell you about our little disagreement?"

"He said you quit after a fight of some kind," Caroline said. "Something about how the paper should be run."

George grinned. "It was a fight, all right," he said. "I'd been getting more and more pissed off with the way we pay our people. Take Virg here, for example. Look at this apartment! He's living in the Aldean slums. If he took a job with the *LA_Times*, or the *Chronicle* in Frisco, he'd literally triple his salary overnight. He's just hanging around here because, like the rest of the males in town, he likes to look at Caroline."

She blushed again, and Virg was looking indignant and shamefaced, but didn't say anything.

"I don't mind," George continued, "because I've got some other income selling my photos to suckers who think it's art. But look at the folks in the press room. Look at the girls—Sally, and Mary, and Roberta, and Alice. No, forget about Roberta. She works for fun and doesn't need the money. But the rest of them are hurtin', and deserve to be paid right. So like I say, I was pissed off, and Tuesday I decided to get off the pot and do something. I told Bill how everybody was sufferin', and that I knew damn well he could afford to pay more, and said he had to give Virg and the girls and the folks down in the plant a big raise."

"Not a very diplomatic approach," I said.

"I always leave my striped pants home," George said. "Bill said running the paper wasn't any of my business, and to get the hell out of his office. And I told him he was right, but that if he didn't come through with more money for the deserving, I would make it my business. And he asked how I thought I could do that. And I said by organizing the *Weekly Aldean* branch of the National Newspaper Worker's Union." At this point George paused and gave us his wicked and devilish grin. He kept us in suspense only for a moment, then added, "And at that point Bill said I was fired."

CHAPTER 16

Ten Months Later

Emil sailed as a boy, and he taught me bowlines and bights and rudders and sheets when our children were young and we had a boat of our own a few years. So I knew all about yachting folk and their hard drinking that always goes with cordial welcoming hospitality. Three weeks of friends we'd made along the sea in Georgia but no glimpse of what we came for. Emil's impatience was groping around like a maze mouse that wants out but doesn't know how to ask, and we were out of Savannah driving into South Carolina before he got plaintive.

"Abigail," said he, "how long are we going to keep at this?"

Patting his knee said I, "Until he's found, here or Alabama or Florida since it wasn't Georgia."

"Maybe we're wrong," said he. "Maybe he's in Europe after all. Or maybe somewhere else—maybe South America, or the South Seas."

His "we're" wrong was sheltering what he was thinking my mistake, for the trip was all my doing. "No," said I. "Somewhere here. Just around the bend of the next river or anchored behind yonder island."

The police and FBI hadn't found Bill Bowman disappeared. I don't know they'd looked very hard, since he'd paid all his taxes, and no one claimed Charlie Ryan's estate, and Europe was out of everyone's bailiwick so looking was unthanked trouble. But they should look he had forged Ryan's name and stole his money and got a false passport. I kept phoning George and Virgil and Sadie, and still saw worry there in La Aldea. Caroline did and didn't own the paper. Jill and David no alimony, so she was too poor for a mortgage sold the house, and he planning scratching out extra jobs for college. Bill wasn't a man to fret over loose ends, and left a mess behind probably not even thinking.

So I thought about it and told Emil a vacation so as to get the muddle unmuddled.

"And just how are we going to do that?" said he.

"He'll make troubles right when he knows 'em," said I.

"You really think he'd help them all," said he, "Caroline, and David and Jill, if he knew the hard time they're having? What makes you so sure?"

"He's a most moral man," said I, "and it's wrong Jill sold her house."

"Oh, I'll concede he's a great one for insisting that *others* do right and shun wrong, but he doesn't apply the rules to himself. He always does what's best for him, and then whatever it is, it's right."

"Jill's alimony," said I.

"You mean what he agreed to when they divorced? Well, he was generous, all right. At least, generous for a publisher of a small-town newspaper. But not for a multi-millionaire. And besides, when he left Jill he knew he'd be retiring and going to Europe in a few years. Probably he figured he'd stop paying then."

"Conscience runs with ethics," said I. "Sleep's hard when you've done wrong."

"Well, maybe so. Certainly when we first met Bowman I thought he had a conscience, but now . . . ? Anyway, it's a moot point. Where are we going to find him? You want to gallivant around all over Europe looking in stray bars asking whether Mr. Bowman has stopped in lately? *Pardon, m'sieur. Avez-vous vu M. Bowman, le grand impersonateur?'*

"You're silly sarcastic," said I, "and your Frenglish foul. Not Europe because we'll find him here in the South living on the shore with a sailboat and a girl."

"And what have you been putting in your cranberry juice that makes you think a thing like that?" he asked.

"He loves boats and the sea but only has English, and those last two years he made two trips to Atlanta, a week each time but no travel receipts at the paper."

He looked at me frowning. "You went back to La Aldea to check travel receipts?" and I nodded. "And on that tenuous foundation of fact you're building a skyscraper of inference that'll have us chasing stray sloops in Georgia? As I remember, he loves big cities as well as the sea. He wouldn't have any trouble learning Greek or French or Hindu. And he probably went to some kind of newspaper convention in Atlanta."

How can you persuade an engineer who only sees what he's been thinking, but I tried. "I checked. No newspaper meetings. It's a lot of bother to learn a language. And the ocean has had him since years and years. Besides, he let the world think Europe with Swiss money and telling Caroline Greece, so no one imagines he's here."

He weakened a little, a small boy asking what's for dessert after he's told the third time to eat his spinach and salad and liver. "And how do you propose we proceed, looking for him, supposing we go off on this daft trip to the wilds of Dixie?"

"Guessing gives up to reason so you tell me," said I. "We start he bought a boat last Fall on the coast from Atlanta."

"Probably hundreds of people did that," said he. "Maybe thousands, I don't know. Well," he gave up because he doesn't care to argue me and remembers the times I'm right, "we're due for a vacation, and I don't have any business lined up. Besides," with a leer and an arm around me and a friendly grope or two, "it's nice travelling with you because you always pack sexy nightgowns you seldom wear at home. When do you want to leave?"

I gave him a friendly grope right back and a kiss to go with it to tell him he was a nice man to give in, and we left a week later.

In Atlanta an old Emil friend, big wheel bossing computers for the state, persuaded his machines to print all sailboats thirty feet long or more registered new in Georgia from July to December last year. No Bowman's or Ryan's there, and none of the boats the Faraway like his sloop in California, and not any Wideapart's, or Longago's, or Nearathand's or such names might remind a whimsical man of past times. But of course Bill was smart enough to get away, and wouldn't be foolish with his new names. So we and the list drove down to the coast and started the hunt with my hair in a braid and Emil an unaccustomed hat and both of us sunglasses, so we could see him before he knew us.

We were sailors maybe retiring and buying a boat, starting down at St. Marys, and met every boat dealer and saw all the anchorages and landings and yacht clubs and anywhere a boat could be. All the computer list names we checked one way another, but no Bill Bowman. Maybe he missed the list, likely changed his name so we tried other things too. Met a lot of fine and friendly folks but no luck otherwise, and now we were starting Carolina without even computer help because Emil didn't have a friend here.

First stop Hilton Head was the way they all were. We began with sellers found in the Savannah library Sunday classified "Boats for Sale" of last year's Charleston and Columbia papers. Two of those were local, for Emil to call.

"Hello," he said on the phone to the first. "My name's Johnson. Were you the one who offered the sailboat last September? Yes? Sounded just like what we were looking for. Is it still for sale? No? Maybe the new owner's looking to sell it himself now. Who'd you sell it to? Dick Urell, you say? If he's a married man with a lot of kids, maybe the family is tired of the boat by now. Three kids, huh? And all enthusiastic sailors, last you saw of them? Well, I guess it's a lost cause. But thanks very much for your help."

At the second local number the buyer was a bachelor too young for Bill Bowman, so we gave up our classifieds a while and looked up the local boat people in the yellow pages to go out snooping. First stop was boat broker Harvey Fothingill whose office was his home or his pocket, and in he invited us to nautical furnishings and sailing ship paintings. Emil introduced us and said, "We're sailors thinking about moving to these parts, though we don't have definite plans yet. Could we buy you a cup of coffee and get your advice about local conditions—where people keep their boats, and what kind of services are available, and how many sailboats are around and is there a local sailing club and so on?"

"I'd be delighted to tell you about Hllton Head," said Mr. Fothingill, "tell you all about it and it won't even cost you a coffee," taking us into the kitchen.

"It's not really fair, our using up your time," said I. "We're a long way from deciding what to do and buying a boat from you or anybody."

"Now my wife's passed away, left me behind, it's always nice to visit with strangers," said he getting out some cups, "especially strangers with pretty wives. Cream and sugar?" There was a big pot of coffee already made and he looked at us bright-eyed, must have been over seventy and mahogany brown. So we took the coffee and sat ourselves around the kitchen table. "It's a lovely place here," said he, "a perfect place for sailing. You can head out to sea, to be on your own, by yourself with the gulls, or just cruise up the bays, sail around the harbors exploring the scenery. We've a local sailing club that plans regattas and parties, but there's no club-house, no place permanent; we just meet at members' houses."

"We'd probably be buying a thirty-foot boat," said Emil. "Are there many around that size or bigger? Or do most people have smaller boats for racing and fun?"

"We have a mixture," said he, "a blend. Mostly day sailers, but quite a few your size, yawls and sloops and schooners."

"Do you have a boat yourself?" said I.

"Just a small one, just a sailing dinghy," said he. "Sold the Columbia, got rid of it after my wife was gone. 'Twas no fun sailing that big boat without her. Kept rememberin' the good times, the times we laughed in the wind, heeled over and legs braced. She'd never been on a boat when we married, but she learned fast and loved it, in the end. Loved it. I hope the Good Lord takes her sailing sometimes, nowadays."

"There's always a fair breeze in heaven," said I. "Has she been gone long?"

"Twenty-three years, this coming September," said he a lonely man a long time. "Two-hundred and seventy some odd months." He'd not got over it nor ever would. Some recover like a hailstruck farmer planting a new crop, and some don't an ancient oak split by lightning.

"Was she a native of Carolina?" said Emil.

"Indiana," said he. "She was a Hoosier. A Hoosier, and I met her on a business trip when I was selling hardware, a long time ago. Thirty years married, and now twenty-three alone." He shook his head to clear it of old thoughts. "But let's get back to your questions. What else can I tell you?"

"Well, where do folks keep their boats?" said Emil. "When outsiders come in and buy one and don't know a soul, are they able to find a place to tie up, or an anchorage?"

"Not easy to find a berth, or slip, unless you buy a house along the bay, the harbor. But there's plenty of anchorage space. If you buy something locally, you want to try to get the rights to its mooring, if you can."

"Would a couple of Californians like us have any trouble joining your sailing club?" said I. "Have you had many strangers come in the past year or so, and have they fit in all right?"

"You'd be mighty welcome," said he. "Mighty welcome, though we don't get all that many people from out-of-state. Last one I remember was Henry Braun. He and his family, four nice kids, you'd like 'em, got here around . . . oh, around eighteen months ago, from Alabama. Joined the club first thing, and're very popular. No, you'll fit in just fine. Just fine. Now how about I take you out and show you around. You can't get a feeling for a place without you walk it or sail it, without you see it."

We agreed, and around we went the town and the county. We met club members, and admired boats for sale, and visited ship hardware stores, and looked anchorages, and turned down invitations to sail that afternoon, and took lonely Mr. Fothingill lunching. Nowhere heard of anyone could be Bill Bowman, but we made some more new friends and left inviting Harvey we'd take him sailing in California.

That night was Beaufort where Emil remembered he'd been when the Marines had him at Parris Island World War Two. The Stockade he said was where he learned being an electrician, living under canvas and mosquitoes and eating out of mess gear standing up in a hot tent. I couldn't tell was he the old soldier bragging, or the hurt child knuckling his eyes for sympathy. But we kept at the hunting the next day and heard about two newcomers worthwhile. Both were the right age, had no families, and bought big boats late in the year. One was easy, sold insurance and we walked by his office saw him in the window, skinny and blond. The other seemed very promising because of his name, Bill Beeson, but he was harder to check. We looked his address on some papers over the shoulder of the boat broker mentioning him, but he didn't answer his phone and we couldn't find where he worked. Finally located him in a bar with a redhead near where his boat anchored, and he wasn't Bowman either.

The next few days were much the same, full of questions with answers that led up blind channels and down dead bayous, and we checked into Charleston Friday evening tired. Saturday morning we phoned the advertiser list and found three bachelors the right age had bought boats, but only got the address of one, didn't answer his phone. Phoning some more trying where their boats might be, and learned that one a ketch *Easy Days* was in a big yacht club just north of town, but nothing more. We put that on our list and climbed in the car to continue calling on strangers pretending we might buy a boat. One of the bachelors showed that morning but he wasn't it, and we heard of four other boat buyers all too young or with big families we were sure weren't Bill. Then in the early afternoon Emil cornered a boat surveyor leaving me inquiring of insurance for a yawl we might buy. Young Mr. Black was very eager and kind, and glad to explain different policies their good parts and drawbacks, and he finished and I pointed the terminal on his desk.

"What's that for?" said I.

"It's a computer," said he inaccurately but I didn't let on what an expert I am, "and keeps records of all our policies."

"How do you use it?" said I. "Can you for example see everybody bought boat insurance from you the past year?"

"Certainly," said he. "Let me show you. These things are amazing." And he banged away at the keys, hitting them brutal thinking the machine only understood fierce frantic fingers. "There," said he. "Seven new customers." I looked at the screen and saw

2/8/87	Everett Wing	North Star
5/22/87	John Midlotts	Amelia
6/5/87	Henry Johnson	Sublime
6/30/87	J.W. Evans	Peachtree
8/28/87	Samuel Poughmone	Easy Days
9/3/867	Edward Davis	Blue Skies
2/14/88	William A. Jones	Spume

"It must be very handy," said I, "business at your fingertips that way. The *Easy Days*. My husband and I heard of her. Sounds like a nice boat."

"It is," said he. "In fact, Bill had it fixed up and is living in it now, over at the club."

"Bill?" said I.

"Bill Poughmone," said he. "His real name's Samuel, but he says he's been known as 'Bill' as far back as he can remember."

"And you pronounce his name 'Poe-man', though it looks it ought to sound like 'Cow-stone'," said I for that's how the *Easy Days'* previous owner had pronounced it over the phone.

He laughed. "Not everybody has easy names like yours and mine, Mrs. Lime. Is there anything else I can tell you about boat insurance?"

I told him no and went out to wait for Emil, soon showing up a big excited smile and said, "I think I may have found him."

"You mean old Sam Poughmone on the *Easy Days*," said I rhyming it with Yeoman. He was disappointed and I was right away sorry, should have let him tell me about it. "That's right. How did you hear? Do you know he's called Bill? And was enthusiastic about yachting, though my surveyor friend said he was surprisingly ignorant about boats and sailing. It's the best lead we've run across yet." I agreed, so we got out the map discovering the best way to the yacht club.

The club itself was new, all glass looking at acres of boats in neat rows, and a big parking lot must be full on the weekends. We took our sunglasses disguises and wandered along the seafront wondering how to see Sam Poughmone without him knowing we were. There were locks on the gates that let you onto the forest of floats where the boats were, and we passed club members with keys, and saw each gate had a listing of the boats and owners. The *Easy Days* was float E slip twelve.

"Wait for me," said Emil. "I'll get the binoculars out of the car."

"No need," said I. "Look. There's telescopes," and I took him a platform nearby where a quarter was five minutes' look over the bay. We invested or donated and

Emil scanned boats but didn't see anything, and his money ran out and I tried another five minutes unsuccessful, and then Emil tried again.

"Float E slip twelve," said he with another quarter. "It must be somewhere around." He looked a while more with a couple of "Aha's" and then, "I'm pretty sure I know which one it is, but from here you can only see the masts. Have a look. I've got the 'scope set on the E sign, and you can see the first slip is number 2 so the sixth is probably him." I had a look and agreed, and we went back to the car for the glasses to see better.

We wandered again, finally finding a place to see the ketch pretty well, but no one aboard we thought so off to lunch. Still nothing after we came back full, and we drove off to a lookout point close by, parking to wait though it was too far the glasses to see who anybody was. Every half hour back for a close look, and at four o'clock Emil's "Aha!" came again and handed me the glasses. In the stern of the *Easy Days* was Bill Bowman with a new beard sunning drinking a long drink with a young woman with fair hair.

"Amazing!" said Emil when I gave him the glasses back. "Just as you said: he bought a boat somewhere near Atlanta, and is living on it with a new girl. How'd you know about her?"

"Bill needs an admiring audience," said I, "and doesn't mind a little affection to go with it."

"Amazing," he said again, and looked at his watch. "It's too late now, don't you think?" We'd long ago talked what we'd do finding him, needing the banks to be open.

"Let's go celebrate and see in the morning," said I, and that's what we did, having champagne with dinner at a fancy place with French name and Southern food, and a little loving before sleep.

In the morning after breakfast and checking out, Emil put the papers in his pocket and we drove to the club. Just after nine o'clock and the *Easy Days* deserted, so we sat in the car waiting. Half an hour and Emil nudged me, and there was bearded Bill and the blond through the gate to the clubhouse. We waited more and in a while they came back. We caught up and took off our glasses and said "Hello, Bill," so he turned and saw us.

There was a second uncertainty, then panic and indecision and white under his tan, then he smiled a big smile and shook our hands. "Abigail and Emil!" said he. "How nice to see you! Marcia, these are Abigail and Emil Lime, old friends from Chicago. And this is Marcia Hunt, who helps me with my boat the *Easy Days*. Come on down and have a look at her," and he opened the gate and let us through. "The only disadvantage to living on a boat is the facilities," he said. We have to do our morning toilets up at the club. How long have you been in town?"

We told him a few days and talked of this and that, and aboard the boat Marcia poured us coffee lounging around the cockpit. In a while Bill said, "We were going grocery shopping this morning," and then, "Marcia, would you mind taking care of it? We'll be conversing about old times which'll be tedious for you. Take my car—it's nearer the gate than yours." Marcia didn't mind, and got her purse and gave Bill a kiss and went off, and Bill looked at us worried and said, "Well. And may I enquire why you've bothered to look me up?"

"There are things in La Aldea that need fixing," said I, "and we knew you would want to put them right when you heard."

He frowned. "I'll be glad to be of assistance if I can. What's the trouble?"

"Caroline and Jill and David are in the lurch," said I, "and we know you have a new life but theirs has to be easier. Emil, why don't you show him?"

Emil took the papers out his coat and handed them to Bill and talked. "We had a lawyer put these together before we left home," said he. "This bunch deeds your personal property—the house and the car and the *Aldean Weekly*—over to Caroline. She'll come into it all eventually, after you're declared presumed dead or something, but that'll take seven years or more."

"Of course," said Bill. "I should have thought of that. I didn't intend that Caroline would be left in difficult straits. How is she, by the way?"

"She's just fine," said I not mentioning she was living with Virgil now very happy indeed.

"And these other papers set up a trust," Emil went on. "You remember the courts awarded Jill alimony," Bill nodded, "and you may have forgotten, but this Fall David wants to start college. You've left them with hardly any savings. The trust will pay Jill's alimony for thirty years, and David's college tuition and expenses."

"And what is it I am to do?" said Bill.

"Sign all the papers," said Emil, "putting your fingerprints down in the blocks indicated. That'll prove it was really you that signed, and we won't need a notary public or anything that will divulge where you are. Then set up the trust with $500,000. You can afford it, since you had over three million dollars in that Swiss account. The money can be in cash, or gold, or securities made out to bearer, or anything you like. You see, we've fixed things so that you'll be able to remain hidden. We won't tell anyone where you are, and the documents and money can't give you away."

"What'll happen when Fred asks how and where you located me?"

"He won't ask. No one will know we had anything to do with this. Caroline and Jill's lawyers will just get these documents, and the securities, in the mail, postmarked New York or Dallas, or somewhere that won't point here."

Bill looked relieved. "That sounds fair enough," said he. "I didn't mean to make life difficult for them all. Leave it to me. I'll attend to it."

"Well, we thought," said Emil, "now that we've come all this way, we'd see the whole thing through. We had in mind you'd sign the documents, and give them and the half-million to us. We'll put them in the mail on the way home."

A minute he thought, then "Sounds as if you don't have confidence in me, but you expect me to trust you with all that cash?"

"We figured you might not want to do that," said Emil, "so an alternative is for all three of us to go to Dallas or wherever you suggest and jointly put the envelopes in the mail."

"Half a million is a lot of money," said Bill. "I don't have access to that much here in Charleston. I'll have to visit New York."

"Then let's go," said Emil. "Let's get the earliest flight we can. With luck we could be in Manhattan today before the banks close. Anyway, we can take care of everything tomorrow."

Bill thought about it doubtful but agreed. We pushed the papers and he signed with his fingerprints too, from a stamp pad Emil had brought. As he signed he cheered up, I figured him thinking it was good to get his conscience cleared, but it turned out I was wrong. He said,

"I never did hear. What were the sentiments of my friends in La Aldea, when they heard of my departure? Did anyone notice the appropriateness of the headline for my last editorial on Ed Hooper: 'Are Things as They Appear to be?' I thought that was a nice touch."

As he spoke, Marcia came down the dock trundling a cart of groceries no time to answer. Bill and Emil helped her get them aboard and put away and Bill said, "How would you like a quick journey to New York, my love?"

She gave him a big smile for 'yes', and he told her to pack and added, "There's a travel agency just across from the club. I'll go buy the tickets, and we'll be off."

Emil got up said he'd go too, and they left. Marcia hadn't talked much, but I asked if I could help pack, so she invited me down and we visited, her putting clothes and stuff In a bag. She had just graduated a small woman's college in Columbia studying English, but the only job was selling boats, where she met Bill. He was a darling but didn't know diddley-twat about sailing, and they read a lot and he was very intelligent didn't I think so, and I said yes and asked about her family.

Half an hour passed after she finished packing, and still no men back with tickets. I began to wonder. Marcia worried too another ten minutes, and then Emil came alone.

"Where's Bill," said Marcia. "I'm all packed."

"Didn't he come back here?" said Emil. He left me at the travel agency saying he had to return for his checkbook. I waited and waited, and then gave up. But I didn't see him as I walked back to the boat. Where could he have gone, Marcia?"

Marcia was puzzled but I was dismayed foolish. I had told Emil Bill was careless but generous not mean, and now he disappeared again I wasn't sure we could ever find him.

CHAPTER 17

That Last Afternoon

The travel agency was like they all are. There were three efficient young ladies who somehow looked to be well-travelled, the three computer terminals they used to capture seats for clients, three much-used telephones, and dozens of brochures touting the charms of distant places. Bowman chose the prettiest of the clerks, and we sat down and asked her about the next plane to New York. There was a flight at noon we could catch, and he told her to fix up the tickets, then reached in his coat and found he had come without his checkbook.

"Wait here just a minute. Emil," he said. "I'll run back to the boat and pick it up—I know just where I left it." He hurried out, and I examined my fingernails and my suspicions. Since learning of Bowman's mendacity, I had not shared Abigail's confidence in his essential goodness, or in the infallible workings of his conscience. That's why I had insisted that we stay with him until everything was signed, sealed, and delivered, though she might have taken him at his word when he said he'd 'attend to it.'

"Excuse me," I said to the young lady after a moment, and hurried out the door myself. Across the street I could just see Bowman in the parking lot headed for the gate to the docks. Maybe all was well, but I still worried a little, and crossed the street myself on the diagonal so if he looked back he'd be unlikely to see me. I walked through some shrubbery and climbed a low fence into the lot, and then suddenly caught a glimpse of him—getting into a car! Keeping my head down, I sprinted in his direction, and arrived just in time to see him leaving in a sporty red Camarro. Luckily our own car was not far away, and I ran to it and took off after him. Got a glimpse of him just leaving the lot, and was able to pick him up right away. I had put on my hat and glasses so he'd be unlikely to recognize me if he looked in the rear mirror, but he had never seen our car anyway, so I figured it unlikely he'd realize he was being followed. He drove soberly, not speeding, and I tried to keep a car or two between us.

He headed into town. I almost lost him when he made a traffic light I missed, but he was stopped at the next one and I caught up. The red car was easy to spot. Mid-town he turned into a parking lot behind a bank, which was pretty much what I had expected. I went 'round the block, then entered the same lot and found a place to park where I could see his car—had a brief shock when I discovered there were two red Camarro's, but I had noted his license number so I knew which was his.

I settled down to wait, reflecting on how slippery and adroit Bowman had been—and evidently still was. In his "farewell" message to Caroline on that last diskette, he had explained how he had needed cash to start his newspaper, and why he'd concluded that Charlie Ryan was dead. But he hadn't told just how he'd set up the impersonation. We'll never know for sure how he worked his swindle, but he certainly took a lot of chances. I wondered how he had reconciled his acts with his moral ideas, when he had pushed off on the hazardous slopes of crime and deception thirty years ago.

He had packed up the deeds and headed east. With Charlie's birth certificate it'd be easy to get a driver's license; but the passport would be another matter altogether—a substantial risk. The real Ryan undoubtedly had one, for he'd been on his way around the world when he'd left La Aldea. So Bowman either found some way to buy a forged passport, or else secured one through the usual government channels. The forgery seemed unlikely, for that would take a wad of cash, and Bowman couldn't have had much money those days. So he must have adopted some sort of disguise which made him look like Ryan. He showed up at an issuing office somewhere, introduced himself as Charlie Ryan, and asked for a new passport to replace the one he'd "lost". He had practiced forging Ryan's signature, but any difference between it and the one on file—or between his new photo and the photo they must have with Ryan's original application—would have to be explained by the number of years that had passed. What had he thought, waiting in that office while the clerks examined his application, and on the subsequent visit when he'd returned to pick up the passport? He'd told Caroline he had convinced himself that Ryan would have left him the properties, had Ryan written a will. So in his mind, he was doing no wrong in selling a La Aldean lot. But surely he knew it was a Federal crime to apply for a passport in a dead man's name. How did he square that crime with whatever conscience he had? What would he have told his parents and his friends in La Aldea, if he'd been caught?

But he'd got away with it, and with passport, driver's license, and birth certificate in his pocket he was ready to introduce himself at the DuPair Bank in New York. He was in a bank in Charleston right now, and I was pretty sure he was closing his checking account and emptying his safe deposit box. He's an old hand by now, I thought, at banking under an assumed name, in some sort of disguise. Every such visit brought a risk of some kind, though none as chancy as the passport application. That time in New York he must have made himself appear to be an expatriate, perhaps an eccentric one to explain his lack of fixed address. He had introduced himself as Ryan, rented a safe deposit box to hold all the deeds, and arranged for one of the La Aldean lots to be sold, giving the banker a letter to be passed on to Valley Realty. And then he'd headed for home.

When the property sold, he'd made another trip to New York to pick up the money—or rather, part of it. Much of it he left, setting things up so the bank paid his taxes. He'd come home with $20,000, and invented his story of a loan from a family friend. When the newspaper started making a profit, he was going to have to pay off that "loan", and wanted to launder the money back into his business. So when he started the paper he'd hired Martin Neare, whom he'd known in college, as an accountant. His bookkeeper had to be someone who wouldn't be sharp enough to perceive the laundering, and it seemed that Neare qualified.

The years passed and the paper was a success, and the rest of the Ryan property appreciated. The inflation of the early Seventies made Bowman a rich man, on paper. And he was ready to retire. He paid another visit to the bank in New York, this time disguised with white hair and a mustache, and started selling off the other pieces of land. Apparently Dubroski got letters from "Charles Ryan" postmarked in Europe at times when Bowman hadn't left the country, but I could see various ways that could be accomplished. If I were doing it, I'd just visit the LA International terminal some afternoon looking for a nice elderly lady on her way to Paris or London or Rome, and I'd give her my letter and some money and a cock-and-bull story, and ask her to post it for me from Europe. However he worked it, Bowman got Dubroski and Tom Valley selling the property. But this time there were millions of dollars coming out of the sales—far too much to launder through the *Weekly Aldean.* So he'd paid his taxes, and moved the balance to a Swiss bank account. Undoubtedly he'd had still another name there, and a new disguise to go with it.

Abigail had suspected something was wrong long before I did, and had figured the culprit was probably Bowman when I was still convinced we should be looking for a confidence man.

"What made you think it was Bill?" I had asked her as we drove home from La Aldea the day Bowman had become a fugitive.

"One feather could be a leaking pillow or a child's treasure," she'd replied. "But fifty scattered around the cat's cushion and you begin to look for the missing bird." And she'd gone on to list the feathers. Some of them just pointed to a La Aldean rather than a stranger—the pun story missing from the diskettes and the library, the choice of Valley Realty, the fact that the most modest of Ryan's properties was the first to be sold.

But there were other things that Abigail felt branded Bowman himself: his self-righteous indignation at Aldean hypocrites; the low wages he paid his reporters and the low clothing allowance he gave to Caroline; his apparently unmotivated divorce; his virtual abandonment of son David. She admitted those factors were pretty inconsequential, really circumstantial indications of character, rather than evidence of guilt. More telling were, first, his founding of the *Weekly Aldean* in 1957, just the time "Ryan" had got $47,000 for the first piece of property; second, his hiring of an seemingly incompetent accountant to keep books for his new paper; and finally, his failure in the 1980s to fight Ryan's sale of the rest of the real estate—Bowman condemned the sale in conversation, arguing that it would ruin lovely, rural La Aldea, but he didn't campaign and editorialize against it in his newspaper.

"But on the whole that's a pretty wispy and unsubstantial bag of quills," I said. "Hardly enough to convict a poor cat."

"The feather just pointed," was her reply. "The fingers convicted." She meant the fingerprints.

Of course, if the body hadn't been found, if the ring hadn't been found with it, if the story of the finding hadn't appeared on the wire services, if old Somers Grant hadn't put the ring in his pun story, if Bowman hadn't hired me, if I hadn't noticed the missing stories on the diskettes, if Virg hadn't been looking for a story he vaguely remembered . . . . if a lot of unlikely things hadn't occurred, Bowman would still be back in La Aldea, looking forward to a luxurious retirement as himself, with lovely Caroline. Instead, here he was in an elaborate disguise with an insipid blonde. And it looked as if he was going to disappear again.

It was about fifteen minutes before he came out of the bank carrying a bulky envelope. He locked it in the Camarro's trunk, got into the car, and headed out of the lot. I waited a moment, then followed. I didn't know the city very well, but in a few minutes I could see he wasn't headed back to the yacht club. It looked as if he was going to leave Marcia as he'd left Caroline. What could I do? He might drive for hours before he stopped for the night. I couldn't very well follow him in those circumstances. Of course, I had his license number. I'd just find out what direction he was headed, then return to Abigail. If she agreed, we could go to the police, tell them we'd located a fugitive from justice, and give them the license number and a description of the car. Or maybe she'd have a better idea on how we could catch up with him.

He stopped alongside a city park, and I found a place to wait and watched him go into a drug store, then to the men's room in the park. When he came out he had shaved his beard and was wearing a baseball cap—a new disguise, and I almost didn't recognize him! Then he stood by the curb; and I noticed it was a bus stop. The bus came and he got on, leaving the Camarro there by the park with his envelope in the trunk. I followed the bus, and after a twenty-minute ride he got off by a used car dealer. So he was going to buy a car. He'd left his red car and taken the bus because when they found the Camarro they'd never be able to connect it to his new one bought from a dealer some distance away. But of course he'd go back to pick up the envelope which I was pretty sure contained three million dollars worth of securities.

At the car dealer he found a salesman, and began looking at cars. He was going to disappear in his new beardless disguise, undoubtedly with a new name to go with it. But he'd given me the chance I was looking for, and so I did what I hoped I'd be able to do, and then returned to the yacht club and Abigail and Marcia. I didn't want to tell Marcia what had happened, so I explained that Bill had left me waiting for the airline tickets, saying he had to get his checkbook.

Marcia was surprised, but had no idea where Bill could have gone. Abigail was abashed, thinking we'd lost him, but after a bit I slipped her a reassuring wink, and her anxiety was replaced by curiosity.

We waited another half hour with no sign of Bill, and then told Marcia he must have changed his mind about the New York trip, and that we had to go. We gave her our home address and told her to have Bill call us when he returned. She was beginning to look a little worried. She would certainly be mystified if she never saw Bill again, but I had a hunch he'd change his mind and come back.

As we walked back to the car, Abigail took my arm and said, "Tell me why he's gone and you're not worried enough."

I told her how I'd followed him—about his going to the bank and shaving off his beard and winding up buying a car. "And so," I finished off, "it was clear he was going to disappear again, and I wasn't sure we'd be able to catch up with him. But he's signed the trust and the deeds, and all we need are the securities. We don't need Bill himself. So while he was buying the car, I drove back to the Camarro, opened the trunk, took out most of the contents of his envelope, and came on back."

"He left the trunk unlocked with all the money?" Abigail asked.

"Oh, no. He locked everything up tight. But I had a key."

"A key? Where . . ."

"I borrowed Marcia's keys while we were loading the groceries onto the boat. Dropped them back in the galley just now as we left."

"That was a fine farthing's fragment of foresight worthy of a seer who knew he'd want to open Bill's car trunk."

"I didn't know, of course. But also I didn't have your faith in Bill's decency, and thought it might be useful to have the keys. I must admit I was figuring we might want to use them to get into the boat rather than his car, though."

She thought for a minute, and sighed. "I don't know what else you could have done, to get us the half-million for Jill."

"More than that," I said. "I made off with more than that. It seemed to me Bill needed a lesson in generosity. So I figured we'd help him make a big contribution to the Red Cross and the Cancer Institute and the Salvation Army, and I left him just about $100,000 with which to resume his carefree life. I've got over three million dollars worth of government notes and IBM and General Electric and other stock in the back of the car."

"Emil! That's not what we said we'd do! What right have we taking all his money?"

"We're not taking it. We're distributing it for him, partly to Jill and David, and partly to deserving philanthropic organizations. It's not what we said we'd do, but then Bill didn't do what he said *he'd* do."

"Why didn't he come back?"

"When he found the money missing, you mean? Probably he hasn't noticed yet. I stuffed his envelope with road maps, so it's still about as bulky as it was when he left the bank."

"Very sneaky but still he could have opened it."

"If he had, he had no way of knowing I was the thief. What could he do? Call the police? He's in a bind, you see. I figure that when he opens the envelope tonight or sometime and finds only $100,000, he'll think about it for a while, then figure he has to return to Charleston because of the boat. It must be worth $25,000 or so. If you have almost three million dollars, you can carelessly throw away a $25,000 sailboat when you disappear. But when you only have $100,000, that $25,000 looks like a lot of money. So probably Marcia'll see him again. Whether he'll stay in Charleston, or go off and make a new life somewhere else—who knows?"

"If he finds Jill with trust money he'll know we were thieves."

"That's right. But how will he find out? And if he does, what can he do? We'll endorse the securities over to the charities, forging Charlie Ryan's name on them. And we'll ask them to send receipts to Ryan care of Mr. Samuel Poughmone, in Charleston. So Bill will know what happened to his dough. I don't think we'll ever hear from him again."

Abigail and I caught a two o'clock plane to Washington, where we spent the night. The next day we bought some sturdy envelopes and put all our documents and securities in the mail, addressed to the proper parties. The day after that we flew home.

*   *   *

Our Aldean friends were surprised and delighted with their unexpected 'gifts by mail'. I'm sure the Red Cross and Salvation Army and so on were, too. Three months have passed now, and Abigail and I are busy with other things. But Abigail still keeps in touch with La Aldea. Caroline has filed for a divorce, and she and Virgil are engaged, and will be married next summer. The *Weekly Aldean* continues prosperous with Virg as editor. George is back taking pictures for it, and the staff is paid more generously these days than it was in Bowman's time. David will go to Princeton this Fall, as will Elizabeth. Ed and Florence Hooper are reconciled, though we hear it is an uneasy truce. Jennifer Able soon tired of Archie Whitmore, and is keeping company with a sensible and diligent rancher. Since no Ryan heir ever showed up, there has never been any trouble about the ownership of the property Bowman sold in Ryan's name; but Tom Valley still worries about it, and says he can't stand the heat and will retire next year. No one believes him.

I was wrong about Bowman, though—we *did* hear from him.

Abigail was glad to see the letter. She figures It explains his second disappearance, though I don't think the acts of that thoroughly dishonest man need any explanation. "He's an idealist," she said, with a typically Abigailian apology, "so Ideas come before everything and the idea of his own deserving was stronger than the idea of Jill's and David's." Apparently he returned to Charleston when he finally looked in the envelope. Heaven knows what he said to Marcia and other friends about his missing beard, but he's Inventive. He thought of something. And he'll always have something to hide behind, whether he's clean-shaven, stubbled, furry, or shaggy. It's the nature of the man. Here's his letter. It came in an envelope postmarked Atlanta, had no return address, included no salutation, and was unsigned.

"The Fifth Amendment to the Constitution states that private property may not be taken without just compensation. Your confiscatory theft of my securities is thus a direct violation of the most fundamental law of our land. In addition, this completely unjustified act has caused manifold difficulties, not only to me, but to other Innocent parties. I have been forced to sell my boat. Marcia has been deprived of a friend and sailing companion, and has been permanently hurt. The club has lost a valuable member, along with the *Easy Days'* substantial slip rental. Several Charleston merchants are owed money that Samuel Poughmone was unable to pay. Poughmone himself has disappeared, to the dismay of his many friends and acquaintances. And I have been forced to leave a comfortable, pleasant, and beneficial environment, and must seek a new and undoubtedly less pleasant means of living. How could I remain in Charleston, knowing that my "friends" the Lime's, who had cheated me of my earnings, might also renege on their promise not to publish my whereabouts?

What possible right had you to cause so much trouble to so many people? Why in heaven's name didn't you leave it to me to fund the trust, and take care of Jill and David? Didn't I acknowledge my oversight as soon as you pointed it out to me? Didn't I say I'd provide for them—didn't I tell you to leave it up to me? Who are you to decide what should be done with my capital? To give it away to undeserving charities? For thirty years I worked diligently and conscientiously, creating, in the *Weekly Aldean*, a responsible, vigorous, entertaining, and eloquent force for good in California society. Am I not entitled to a pleasant and comfortable retirement in return? Should I not be rewarded for my labor? For the brilliance of my ideas, and for the chances I took? For my investments in time, in concepts, in travel to far places?

Certainly I deserve better than has been given me. And you two meddling interlopers, interfering in things that are none of your business, have deprived me of my rights. The world is unjust. I have been done in by a boorish, uncultured, Philistine computerist and a muddleheaded, lame brained, incoherent busybody, and I hope the two of you will rot in Hell."

As you can see, he was an "eloquent force" right up to the last we heard from him. And you'll find in the next and final chapter, our sturdy, articulate, vehement ex-editor continued to enthrall the innocent and the self-righteous, writing about the perfidious and the deceitful. The world being what it is, he has plenty to write about.

1992

CHAPTER 18

Home is where the heart love life is and now years after
Bill Bowman and La Aldea. Worse than I guessed, he was,
trying to escape Emil with the money and then writing
bitter words. But always thinking he's right, an idealist with
ideas struggling against the good and moral.

Yesterday, David Bowman found us easily we never
move. After hellos came "Mrs. Lime, I'm married now and
have a son. My mom remarried, so I have a stepfather who
dotes on the boy; but my wife Rose thinks he should meet
his real grandfather. Do you suppose you and Emil could
find him?"

"Last I heard your father was a leper pariah," said I.
"You've changed your mind, then?"

"Time passes," he replied, "and I still think what he
did was shameful. But my sweet wife has a point, and I'm
willing to try to get along with him."

Good he has a sweet wife and says it. "Finding is not
what he wanted," said I. "Maybe there's no way but I'll talk
to Emil and let you know."

Emil just on his way to Chicago business tripping said I
could go ahead probably not possible. I phoned told David
I'd try it a whirl and thought: Bill Bowman knows only
newspapers so he's started part-time reporting for some small
or big paper. Small he's editor now. Big, he's off-dashing
Opinions and Editorials so readers'll know what to think.
A new name and a new lady but still his old hypocritical

self says one thing believes does another. Thinks he's a sage visionary so likely a big paper hoping expecting a local reputation out of sight.

The La Aldea paper weekly, only local news. In a big paper then hypocrisy aimed at the day's big news: at local murder and schools, at national politics or tornados, at world regime change or terrorists. So buy study big city papers with fiery editorialists a dreary tedious job but I'm brimming with idle time.

The library tells the 50 biggest New York, LA, Chicago, Philly, San Diego, Detroit, down to Miami will keep me busy for years. Not likely California or the south so I bought New York, Chicago, Philly, Phoenix, Houston, Detroit, Dallas for starters.

The first two weeks finding my way like the blind lady in the Brailless library. Dreary reading headlines of disaster horror fraud with 'human interest' babies and pets. Then the comics to lighten up but keep your eye on the ball, Abigail. Why so little good news happy families, 75th anniversaries, beautiful gardens, first jobs, first house? Boring?

Some papers had photos of editors not what Bowman would allow but I looked anyway. Main trouble editorials not signed. Needed several with same indignant style so buy papers every day and hope disgruntled heat would upturn. Several days times several papers is a lot of reading so I looked and looked feeling lucky editorials only not the classifieds and fashions and sports.

Emil home took him to bed before he put down his suitcase like the old joke. Delightful loving slept late the next morning. At breakfast I told him where I thought he was.

"I figure writing editorials in a big city newspaper," said I telling the cities I picked. "Four weeks each paper groping for sarcasm, society evils, world at risk, good workers and bad businessmen, endangered daisies and turtles and such stuff."

"Any luck so far?"

Philly has "'Country on wrong track', 'Immigrants deserve respect', 'Higher taxes essential'. Detroit has 'Builders threaten warbler habitat', 'ACLU sues to protect protestors', 'County employees denied raises'"

"Sounds promising," said Emil. "So what have you done to see if Bowman wrote that stuff?"

"I need ideas suggestions. Called the *Los Angeles Times* editors as an example and they won't tell who wrote what claiming all editorials joint by many people and I figure other papers will say the same. Papers print the names of some reporters editors but not all of them."

"We could visit the cities I suppose," Emil said, "and make some informal inquiries. Make the acquaintance of an editor or publisher and do some discreet probing. But that would be expensive. How can we narrow down the search, do you suppose?"

"Narrowed searches seem difficult," said I. "Maybe my genius husband will think invent something in a while."

On we went for weeks with other cities and Emil helping when he was home not off businessing. Once he consulted in Indianapolis where there were likely editorials.

"I went to the newspaper office," he reported, "and noticed a couple of secretaries." That's my husband bet he picked the pretty ones with slim waists. "Waited outside at quitting time and followed one of them. But she got in a car, and I couldn't follow, so I went back to the office and luckily saw the other one. She went shopping and I followed and struck up a conversation." He's not a hunk, my husband, but he somehow charms the girls being shy.

"Her name was Sylvia and I told her I was a detective and invited her for a drink. She had never met a detective, so she agreed. I bought us a couple of beers, and said my client wanted to hire a forward-looking reporter like the one who wrote . . . . And I told her the titles of the editorials we'd found. Did she know who wrote them, and could she tell me?

"She could and did, but they were written by three different people, a girl and two guys. I got the name of the men and she told me the name of the bar where they could be found. So after telling her goodbye I went to the bar. One of the guys was there, and he wasn't Bowman. The next day I went to the newspaper office and found the other reporter and he wasn't Bowman either. So we struck out."

Back to the papers and weeks later more cities and some likely grumblers we put on our list getting pretty long now. Emil's consulted two more cities with possible Bowmans but no luck both times.

One Boston paper editorials extremely good with 'Murder shows need for better gun controls', 'Raise taxes on the rich', 'No oil drilling off the coast', 'U.S. still a racist society', 'Government should ban huge business bonuses', 'Teacher's Unions need support' surely sounded like Bowman. Plane to Boston and a room and next day to the paper. Got to the editor Harry Brown a charming man by showing a little leg. Then blinked my eyes a small flirt and said I was Abigail Lemonlight from Santa Monica and how much I admired his paper all its support of important causes. He preened a little wanted to take me to lunch.

At noon a small café not far away a table for two we got acquainted. His wife had left him and I said I widowed with a trust fund wanted to invest champion worthy causes. We talked children and hobbies and travels half an hour then

I wondered about sitting in an editorial meeting to learn how articles came to be. He was happy to and back to the office a big room with a window looking on the town. He introduced me a dozen men and women no Bowman here and I admired the gun control and tax the rich and no oil drilling and wondered who wrote them. Most by a pretty woman happy to be complimented but all writers were there so I gave up. After the meeting thanks and avoiding dinner with Harry and back to the hotel.

Going home stopped at Oklahoma City another paper with advanced principles but no Bowman there either.

More newspapers and another month and then a break came along like a lottery win for a penniless urchin. A columnist named Joseph Patterly on the big *Honolulu Herald* wrote a story every week and all of them sounded like Bill Bowman worried about the world's unfairness. No photo of Joseph though most columnists like their pictures showing them charming and thoughtful. Emil away so when he returned proposed a short holiday on beautiful Waikiki promised I'd bring my blue bikini shows almost everything. He figured out why and read the columns and agreed.

The following week a fine hotel on the beach me bikini he body-surfing the next morning his favorite only sport not counting love. He showered and we snuggled and then to the *Herald* office with our dark glasses for disguise. A coffee shop hid us while we waited and lunched and mid afternoon there came Bowman brass-bold and a new moustache back to work. Us away to rent a car and then came back for more waiting and at 4:30 he came out looked around. A minute later a blue convertible pulled up with a very pretty blond opened the door and Bowman got in. We followed up through the hills and Kailua on the beach they drove to a comfortable house. We noted the address and back to Waikiki called David and reported success and his father's address. No "Joseph Patterly" in the phone book so he was unlisted.

David sounded happy said he'd talk to Rose and call back. An hour later he told us he and Rose and the boy would fly over the next day asked if we'd wait for them so we said 'yes' not knowing why and had dinner and bed.

Airport next afternoon to find David and Rose boy in her arms.

"Rose, these are Abigail and Emil Lime," said David.

"David has said such nice things about you. And clearly he's right since you found his father. How'd you do it?"

"We'll tell you the story on the way to the hotel," said Emil. "But we wonder why you want us along when you go to see Bill. We'll just be fifth wheels. And he was never happy with us discovering he stole the money." Not mentioning our finding him making away with all his cash and then his acid complaining letter.

It was Rose who replied. "*I'm* the fifth wheel. He's never met me. And I thought it would be better if he saw other old friends, and that you could explain how you found him." Hugged the boy. "This is David junior, by the way."

Very sweet young lady as her husband had said, so we found their bags and told our story on the way to the hotel. They checked in and rested and an hour later out the hill road to Kailua knocked on the door.

The young blond lady distraught panicked tears at the door.

"May we speak to Mr. Patterly," said David. "I'm his son."

"He's gone," was the reply. "Two men said they were from the FBI came yesterday and took him away. Said he was wanted for forgery and stealing money and filing a false passport. What does it mean? Joe couldn't have done those things."

She let us in to explain comfort.

"Are you my stepmother?" David asked.

"No," she replied. "We're not married. We met and fell in love and have lived together for over two years."

That's Bill Bowman taking advantage no shame embarrassment Caroline then Marcia in Charleston and now another girl.

"We'll try to find him and get him released," said Emil, and we said goodbye went away.

"No coincidence us and FBI finding him," said I.

"I agree," said Emil, "but don't see how it could have happened."

Back to Honolulu the FBI office big fancy building. In the lobby a receptionist Emil said,

"We understand Joseph Patterly was arrested yesterday. Could we talk to someone about him?"

Half an hour and escorted to the second floor small green room handsome chap blue suit modest tie greeted got another chair sat us down named himself as Jason Diamond. Demoralizing if all FBI agents look the same dress the same talk the same but probably not.

"We're trying to find my father," said David. "His name is Bill Bowman, though he was writing under the name of Joseph Patterly."

"We've been looking for him for a long time," said Diamond, "and I guess we must thank the Limes for finding him for us."

"How did we do that?" I asked.

"Well," he replied, "the Boston office got a call from a newspaper editor who said he had been talking to a lady named Abigail Lemonlight from Santa Monica about some editorials, and that when she had left he was a little suspicious and discovered no one by that name had stayed in any Boston hotel and that name didn't appear in any Santa Monica directories. So he thought she might be doing some kind of scam, and he'd decided to let us know.

"The local FBI staff passed it on to Washington, and when a clerk searched for Abigail and newspaper and editor in our data base, we turned up Abigail Lime and Bill Bowman. We had a file on Bowman set up in 1988 because he had stolen some money and forged a man's name and used a false passport. You two were in the file, too, so we wondered what you were up to and suspected you were trying to find the damn crook.

"They assigned an agent in Los Angeles to keep track of you, learned you came here to Honolulu, and let me know. We followed you out to Kailua yesterday, and when you left we just stopped in and picked up Bowman."

"We were trying to find him so he could meet my wife and see his grandson," said David. "Is he here? Could we just see him for a few minutes?"

"He's here right now," said Diamond. "He'll be on his way to Washington soon." He thought a minute. "I guess you could see him for a few minutes, if you like."

So the three Bowmans went to meet the one Bowman we'd see them in the lobby downstairs later and I felt bad guilty.

Emil knew what I was thinking. "Not your fault," said he. "It's David's. If he hadn't asked us for help the FBI would never have found him."

"Let's steal him away get him loose," said I. "I trapped him so I should untrap."

"But he really is a criminal, Abby. He forged Ryan's name, and stole his money and used a false passport. He *should* go to jail."

"The money he lost you stole it back remember?" said I, "so it's just false passport and the FBI sneaking following Abigail Emil. They fooled us we fool them."

"Well, I see your point. But get him away from the FBI?!!! Are you crazy? We'll go to jail ourselves!"

"Stealing a prisoner we've never but there's always a first time like a first child job prize hurricane garden earthquake. First rescue sounds good. Airport maybe a good place."

"Abigail, it's impossible! He'll be shackled to an agent! There may be two agents! How can we possible get him loose?"

"Needs thought," said I, "to get around a guard. Maybe Rose and I flirt him away or you flirt her away. Meanwhile we buy a bolt cutter should do any handcuff."

Time passing brought Rose and the two Davids happy to have seen the father grandfather but sad he was clutched by the FBI. Back in the car Emil horrified protesting I talked rescue and plans and handcuffs to the hotel.

In David's room Rose with little Dave in bed and "We're going to free your father, David" said I. "Rescues are not easy but Emil is amazing ingenious makes the difficult seem simple trouble-free who would have thought it possible."

Emil objected and I turned a deaf ear and a blind eye David hesitating but thought FBI unfair so agreed.

"Two places possible. If his flight changes planes Los Angeles, we have many friends glad to help though we would have to plan quickly. Otherwise Washington when he flies in. Or later comes to trial, gives plenty of time but more difficult. First we must learn when he flies," and I told David how, Emil's protest fading like night music.

David found Washington information number for FBI. "My father has been arrested," said he, "in Honolulu and I hope I can visit him in Washington. Could I find out when his trial will be held?" Delay while operator switched and David explained again giving name Bowman. He listened, then, "So it's too early for the trial date. But maybe I can see him in Washington. Do you know when he will arrive?" Another listen. "And I can arrange a visit when he's there? . . . . Ok, thanks."

"He'll get to Washington early in the morning on Friday," said David. "So that gives us two days to plan." One convert thinks we can rescue, and Emil beginning to waffle waver.

We looked up flights good luck all changed planes Los Angeles two arrived Washington early 6:15 am and 7:00 am, arrive Los Angeles 9:05 pm and 10 pm.

"LA looks good. We don't know which one they'll be on," said Emil now joining the party. "Both layovers are about two hours. So I guess we wait at the airport and see which one your father is on."

We sat and planned and then bed and more plans the next day. Then long phone calls to friends in Los Angeles and the next day flew there.

Thursday evening everything in place Terminal 4 waiting for the first plane. Typical airport planes outside through big windows, people everywhere walking talking running worried happy coming home away on vacation stern businessmen crying babies kids playing. Short wait and there was Bowman last off and cuffed to another husky blue suit. We signaled cohorts ID'd Bowman and followed they settling on a bench to wait we all on balcony in crowd above not together dark glasses hats caps. Soon a young man skinhead sat on bench behind them read a book. Emil had shown himself Bowman saw him knew something was up. An hour husky blue suit FBI bored tired and our henchmen henchlady made their move.

Pretty girl walked by with two men one big one little. They stopped.

"You said he'd be on that United flight," said little man.

"That's what he told me," said pretty girl.

"Dammit, I had better things to do than come here and wait for nothing," said little man collar heating.

"I'm sorry, Hank," pretty girl.

"Sorry does me no good."

"Take it easy, Hank," said big man. "Marie had no way of knowing . . ."

"Keep out of this," said little man furious unexpectedly gave big man a shove.

Things happened fast. Big man stutter-stepped back and crashed into FBI man. Skinhead behind pulled out bolt cutters and dexterously cut handcuffs then ran. Bowman also ran while big man apologizing to FBI and untangling and helping him to his feet and FBI found empty handcuff and pushed big man and looked saw Bowman running. Big man indignant grabbed FBI and asked why he had pushed him he'd apologized and by the time FBI unstuck Bowman and skinhead out of sight.

FBI ran looking for Bowman but Emil had pointed a utility room bag inside with money and clothes. Bowman out of prison clothes into bag clothes and visor cap and back to concourse looking different walking no hurry right past FBI and off to who-knows-where he's an expert on disappearing.

Skinhead to a stretch with no airport cameras ditched the bolt cutter in a trash bin put on a wig removed gloves and sauntered away. Airport cameras couldn't see find him or us disguised on the balcony, and the cutters bought in a second-hand shop by somebody else for cash.

Foolproof plan, FBI furious, Bowman family all happy Emil and I proud peacocks. Might be said only crooks save crooks, but us scofflaws help sons so let FBI help itself.

Next day story in the morning paper front page:

"PRISONER ESCAPES F.B.I.

"Los Angeles, May 15, 1992. At Los Angeles International airport last evening, a prisoner handcuffed to FBI agent Harrison Alliday made his escape. According to witnesses two men and a woman got into an argument near the agent, and one man pushed the other so he fell on the seated FBI man. In the resulting confusion the prisoner somehow got out of the handcuffs and ran.

"The three persons arguing were identified as Marie Witherspoon, Hank Upton, and William Bradton. They were taken into custody and interviewed at the local FBI office, but when we spoke to them after their release, they said it had been an unfortunate incident, that they were sorry, but that they were guilty of no crime. Apparently the FBI agrees.

"The prisoner was Bill Bowman, accused of forgery, of stealing a large amount of money and of lying to obtain a passport. These crimes were committed some time ago, and it's not clear how the authorities found him at this time. He was apprehended in Honolulu and was on his way to Washington, DC, to be imprisoned and tried.

"Airport cameras were of little help. One camera recorded the argument and Mr. Upton's crash into the agent, but was of no help in explaining how Bowman got out of the handcuffs.

"As of now Bowman hasn't been found, though a spokesperson at the local FBI office says it's only a matter of time. She had no comment on how the handcuffs were unlocked or about what steps were being taken to apprehend the prisoner.

"As far as we can learn, this is the first time in history that a prisoner has escaped from FBI custody."

FBI must have looked found bolt cutters but they weren't saying embarrassed to death. Never found our skinhead friend. Agent visited us Santa Monica we told him we'd read of escape how did it happen. He asked where were we on escape day our alibi arranged beforehand no problem so he went away irked discomfited wondering the coincidence escape in the Lime's town.

The young Bowmans said goodbye Rose thanked us glad old Bowman had seen his grandchild. We thought he didn't care another way or one an unsentimental wight now hiding again with a new name new job new pretty trusting naïve young lady.

Celebrated 'first time in history' that night out to dinner at the Montana Street Bistro drank a toast to the FBI then home to bed some rejoiceful loving.

THE END